IF YOU ADORE ME

CIARA KNIGHT

If You Adore Me
Book II
Sugar Maple Series
Copyright ©2020 by Ciara Knight
All rights reserved.

****To receive a FREE starter library (Two free books) AND an alert of Ciara's next book releases, go to Ciara's Exclusive Reader group click here. ****

 Created with Vellum

ONE

"Are you sure those numbers are correct?" Knox studied the graphs and charts and promises of a bright future in front of him. "These numbers are higher than the *Grannies Gone Wild* segment two years ago." He rubbed his forehead and glanced away from the computer screen to find Carissa snuggled into Drew on the old green corduroy couch. They'd become inseparable in such a short time, too short in Knox's opinion. "Hello? Working here."

Drew tore his gaze from Carissa for a millisecond. "Who knew that grandmothers playing poker, riding Harleys, and picking up sailors would've been such a hit?"

Insta-relationships were dangerous. Especially the type that twisted a man's insides and made him vow stupid things. Knox had had that once, the can't-separate-without-feeling-a-pain-in-your-chest kind of obnoxious ache. And he never wanted that again.

He returned his attention to the numbers in front of him. "This is good." Knox tapped his lips with the eraser of his pencil. "No, amazing. Now we can leave this small town of crazies..." He glanced at Carissa and caught her warning glower, but he ignored it and continued. "I just want to get back to the real world, far away from small-town politics. This is the place where people go to settle down. I'm in my prime."

Drew sat forward, adjusting the kitten to his other shoulder, and scooted to the edge of the couch. He let Carissa slip from his arms, but as if too much space between them would shred the man, he clutched her hand and held it to his chest.

Poor love-sick sap. Drew probably rescued that ball of fur from the inn chimney to impress Carissa. Now, he'd be stuck caring for the cat for the next ten to twenty years. Long after this relationship failed. If Drew only knew what happened when he couldn't hold on to her forever.

"You don't get it. The segment on Carissa's bakery has gone viral." Drew glanced at Carissa with the you-are-the-answer-to-everything gaze. "Most of the town's helping fill the orders, and we still need more staff. This doesn't just put your show on the map. It's hit the infamous X over the buried treasure of viewers and patrons. We went from your fledgling career after the scandal of corruption with the car shop to making you a star with baked goods. This is what you've always wanted."

Knox closed the laptop on the antique desk, as if he couldn't face the numbers for fear they would change if he stared at them too long. He'd worked so hard for so long, pouring every ounce of energy he possessed into this business. Hours upon hours, searching for the perfect show all across the country, and he'd found it in this backwoods, backward, tiny Tennessee town. Who would've thunk?

The dead-winter morning wind whistled under the door downstairs. It echoed through the empty old-store space now that the recreation center had completed its repairs and the town elders no longer met there. The building sounded hollow, empty. Like his life.

Self-pity wasn't a trait he coveted, and it was time to move forward. He'd avoided the feelings for years since returning stateside, but this town... It had forced him to slow down, which meant old memories had a chance to catch up. It was time to let go of the past. This was his opportunity for the right future. "We should ride this wave. Let's get on a plane to LA and start organizing the next series."

Carissa cleared her throat, as if announcing she was going to contribute to the conversation even if he didn't like it. "You still have filming to do here. Besides, I thought you and Jackie were getting close."

He shrugged. Jackie, the fashionable member of the five Sugar Maple girl band of lifelong friends, had been fun and had helped kill some time while he was here, but that was all. And that's how she'd wanted it, too. They'd agreed to keep things casual. "We can get a camera crew here in a couple of days. I can film for a week, with highlights of the various town businesses, and then intro into a new series."

No one spoke with words, but based on Drew's and Carissa's side glances and obnoxious nonverbal communication between them, Knox realized he'd missed something. Or he'd chosen not to think about something. He shot up from his chair and paced their small, old apartment-turned-makeshift-office in the center of Sugar Maple purgatory.

After two rounds, he stopped in front of Drew with his arms folded over his chest and his best commanding staredown. "I know you gave your resignation, but I won't accept it. You can fly back here to see Carissa on weekends. Heck, I'll pay to fly you here myself, but you can't abandon ship on me. I need you now more than ever."

Drew let out a long sigh causing the cat on his shoulder to stretch and meow. "I'm not going back to LA except to settle my affairs. I've decided to partner with this town and do my own thing for a while, and you know I have another job lined up that starts in a few weeks. I've lived in Knox Brevard's shadow long enough." He nauseatingly kissed Carissa's hand before continuing, as if he couldn't possibly say another word without connecting with her. Ugh, he had it bad. "That being said, you can't return to LA right now either."

A jolt of warning shot through Knox, but there was no way, no how, he'd be sticking around this tiny Tennessee town full of elder crazies and backyard politics. "Not gonna happen. There's nothing you can say that will change my mind, either." He collapsed in the rickety desk chair, the back gave way, and he flailed his arms like a baby learning to walk to keep himself upright.

"Do you never talk to our assistant?" Drew shook his head.

"Spit it out," Knox demanded.

"Lori negotiated a sit-down to speak to a producer about you doing a show for television. That's right, the big move from Internet to television."

Zaps rapid-fired along his skin as if a thousand tiny explosions detonated.

Carissa kissed Drew on his cheek, retrieved the kitten, and then stood. "I'll leave you two to discuss the details and take Roxy for a nap." She sauntered past Knox as if she owned his future—which, based on Drew's vow to abandon him for a life in Sugar Maple, she did.

The sound of her footsteps and the opening and closing of the front door promised to give Knox five minutes alone with his best friend for the first time in over a week. "Oh my goodness, man. She's really got her hooks in you."

"Stop and choose your words carefully."

Knox held up his hands, knowing Drew was lost in the sea of flipping hair, warm smiles, and soft touches.

Drew grabbed his coat, as if to chase after Carissa before she made it too far away. "You can keep running from life, or you

IF YOU ADORE ME   5

can start living it. If you want to achieve everything that you've claimed you've wanted, then you need to stay here and film these segments. It's just a question of how bad you want it."

The bell over the courthouse rang, as if announcing it was time to move on to his next decision. "I want it, but do I have to sell my soul to the mayor of crazy town to get it?"

Drew tossed a bright-red scarf behind his neck and flipped the end over his shoulder. His face morphed from giddy-school-girl to black-ops dark. "Listen, I know you went through something over there. Some of the men told me there was a woman, and—"

"Nothing to talk about. Just 'cause I don't want to go bake cookies doesn't mean I'm hiding from anything."

Drew shook his head. "I'll see you at dinner in a few hours. We'll talk more then."

"As long as it's about the show. No way you're head-shrinking me, dude." Knox shifted in the possessed chair, and it tipped. He grabbed tight to the edge of the desk for balance. "And as long as it's just the two of us."

"Whatever you say, Knox." Drew gave him a backhand wave, but he paused at the top of the stairs. "Remember the car segment?"

"You promised not to speak about that, ever. I'll never go near a car repair shop again. That's what landed us in the career-crushing pit we had to claw out of."

Drew grinned, the kind that told of his plans that were less than honorable. "I'll see you tonight for dinner. We can talk about everything then. One more thing... The producer is excited about your next segment. Lori says that he's really into it and is flying here with contract in hand for your show. All you have to do is what you do best: host the next segment he chose."

"Done. One more segment, and we're out of this town."

Drew clopped down the stairs.

"Wait, segment he chose? You mean the fashion segment?" Knox hollered after his once-best-friend-turned-lost-puppy, but he was already wagging his tail to get to the bakery. Dang, that boy was in trouble. Knox needed to come up with something to get Drew to realize a woman's promise wasn't fact. More of an intention that might or might not work out.

Images of Alima entering her family home, the trail of silk scarf behind her, pummeled his head. He shot up from the chair, pacing, willing the memories away, but not quick enough. A sharp pain shot through his skull. He doubled over and rubbed his scalp until it subsided. His knees gave way and he surrendered to the floor, where he closed his eyes and waited a few more minutes until the episode passed.

He needed something else to focus on instead of past nightmares. If he had to stay, at least he'd be working with Jacqueline on her fashion. She wanted the fame and recognition more than he did. Hopefully, one more segment would humor whoever this sponsor was, and then he could get out of town.

The sound of steps drew him from his musing, and he realized he was still on the floor. He tried to stand and brush himself off, but his knees weren't cooperating.

Stella, the sassy member of the Sugar Maple girl band, crested the stairs and eyed him with a raise of a brow. "Looking for a colored contact or doing yuppy yoga?"

He wasn't sure if it was the personal attack of her words or just having someone enter a room shattering his tether to the past, but the heart palpitations faded and his legs worked again. With his palm to the hard, cold floor, he pushed up and sat on the edge of the couch to allow his legs another minute to strengthen. So much for recovering at super-speed. He'd been out too long. "I assure you, I don't do yoga and I don't drink seaweed."

"Whatever you say." She shrugged and stood there as if waiting for him to tell her something.

He eyed her oil-stained hands. The odor of old garage filtered to his senses, causing the hair to stand up on the back of his neck. If only he had checked into that car repair company prior to running his segment, he would've discovered they were stealing from the elderly, and he wouldn't have fallen from the top ten Internet show spot into this pool of small town agony. "What dragged you out from under a car and brought you here?"

"I don't want to be here, but I was ordered by my best friend, the one in some love trance that's making her think crazy."

"Can't disagree with you there." Knox scrubbed his face, feeling the slight stubble from his dull razor. "That doesn't explain why you're here now, though."

Stella rolled her eyes, crossed her arms, and huffed. "Because my auto shop is your next segment."

TWO

Knox Brevard looked nothing like the legend. Sure, he was tall, had that sexy, shaggy-yet-kempt hair thing going that rested over platinum eyes. Okay, he also had the broad shoulders and crooked smile. But still, why did people fall all over themselves for celebrities, anyway? Stella waited for Knox to stand and recover from whatever moment of crisis that had taken him to his knees.

He rubbed his temple, as if the idea of working with her was going to split his skull open. "There's a mistake. I wouldn't film you next."

Stella popped her hip out and channeled her grandmother's Latin attitude, God rest her soul. The woman could fling words at someone, causing more damage than a wrench to the head. "You think I'm happy about this? You have no idea how little I want to have to do with you. News flash, you're not even a real celebrity." She turned on her heels and marched out of the room, down the stairs, across town.

She knew too much about the fame-seeking type. They were no better than carburetor-clogging gunk. A useless by-product of hopes and dreams of the impossible that a person sacrificed everything to achieve, even abandoning their own child.

She flung open the door to Sugar and Soul Bakery. At the edge of the display case she'd built for Carissa's bakery, she got friend-blocked by none other than her mentor and second mom to all the girls, Ms. Horton. "Get out of my way." Stella cringed at her tone toward the only real role model in her life. "I need to have a word with Drew and Carissa."

Ms. Horton slipped her arm around Stella's shoulders, despite Stella's well-known no-touching policy, and guided her to the front door. "I'll give them the message, but for now, you need to be at your garage."

Stella slipped from Ms. Horton's motherly comfort. She didn't need it from her own mother, so she certainly didn't need it from her second one. Even if Ms. Horton was the only real mother figure she'd ever known. "I'm not doing it. No way. No how. You go prance around for some show. I'm out."

"Okay," Ms. Horton said flatly.

Stella analyzed this new play. She waited for the next spin, but Ms. Horton didn't add anything.

"What do you mean, okay?"

"I mean that you don't have to do the show if you don't want to, but Carissa told me some man is coming to see your '57 Chevy." She looked at her watch. "In about an hour, so you better get back to your garage."

"Why would anyone want to see my pet-junkyard project?" Stella narrowed her gaze, looking beyond Ms. Horton's crisp ironed jacket, pencil skirt, and authoritative grin.

"Because he's a car guy and he's into classics. I think he needs some work done to one of his cars, too. I assumed you could use the business."

Use the business? Stella's black combat boots were already pointed toward Maple Street. "Why didn't you say so?" She paused her retreat from the bakery, "You're gonna tell Carissa and Drew for me that I'm not doing the show, right?"

"Right," Ms. Horton said with a wave, shooing Stella out the door.

She made it to the stop sign before her hair began to stand up and her gut did that hydraulic-lift thing, warning her she was being managed. But with the frigid temperature and the dangling carrot of garage income–saving work, she didn't have time to interrogate for information.

She shuffled through the sludgy snow along the edge of the road and up the hill until she reached the side street to her garage tucked at the edge of town. Far enough away to stay out of the high-traffic gossip but close enough she could pop into town to help anyone with car issues at any time.

Taped to her garage door was a sign with blood-red writing on it that caught her attention. Her insides gurgled like coolant in an overheated engine. The icy temperatures didn't help the heat racing over her skin. Especially when the writing became legible.

EVICTED.

How could one word cause so much pain and anxiety? Stella forced the rising steam of her temper back into its little hidden compartment she'd learned to store it in over the years. Sure she was hotheaded, but she wasn't combative anymore. Not after the incident that landed her in juvie at fourteen. Despite the system realizing their error when Ms. Horton informed them Stella had been working on her car all day and couldn't have vandalized the school, the memories were enough to scare her straight.

Why would her landlord be calling in her loan now? She'd been behind on payments forever. The avoidance and empty promises had kept him from pressuring her too much. After all, some money was better than none. Who would want to own a failing garage on the edge of a small town besides someone with a family history that bound them to the business?

She pushed away the anxiety and shoved the note in her pocket before about-facing and marching down the street. Thank goodness for Jake. Her walk to his house provided time for her to cool a little. She needed to hurry, though, if she'd make it back in time for the guy coming to look at her Chevy.

The crooked, dark-brown sign that read Hunting and Fishing banged against the front porch. Every day she could hear that sound echo up the street and into her garage. One day she snuck over to fix that blasted sign, but he told her he liked it that way. The old store was actually his belated mother's home that doubled as a seasonal shop.

She knocked, but when he didn't come to the door she turned the old brass knob to discover the door locked. Not much business for hunting and fishing this time of year, unless someone wanted to go ice fishing or something crazy like that. A shadow through the window told her that he was inside, though, so she fisted her hand and pounded on the door three times. "I know you're in there, Jake. Don't be a coward."

The top of his red hair popped up at the bottom of the front window.

"You know I can see you, right?" Stella took in a deep breath and blew it out with a vengeance, expelling all her anger with it the way the counselor had taught her after her father had gone to jail.

"You're not going to hit me?" Jake asked in a whimpering tone.

"My goodness, no. I have a temper, but I'd never hit someone without a good reason. Now open this door so we can talk."

"We can talk through the window, I think." His head rose enough to show his tiny, fear-filled eyes.

"Seriously? You put an eviction notice on the garage and then don't tell me why?"

"I didn't put the sign there. I paid someone to do it. You're behind on payments," Jake said with a little more grit to his tone than she'd expected. She'd been telling him he needed to toughen up or people would walk all over him. Too bad he was using the training against her.

"I know that. And I'm working on it." She tried the knob again, despite already knowing it was locked.

Jake slid below the window again. "You've been working on it for over a year."

A bird swooped down into his dead garden and landed in the tree. A garden that had won the Best Lawn in Sugar Maple four years in a row before his mother passed away. Now he was alone. Obviously lost. Stella could relate. "I know that, but I'll catch up soon."

"No. I won't be a footrest anymore."

Great, he'd thrown her own words back at her. She snugged her hat down and shoved her hands into her jacket pockets. "Why now? I don't understand."

The sparse sprinkling of red hair made another appearance. "Because I have a buyer. Never had a buyer before."

"Buyer? For my garage?" She removed her hands and slapped her palms against the window. "Who in town would want my *abuelo's* old garage?"

"Not a local." Jake's entire head popped up like one of those fun park mallet games she liked to pound her frustrations out on. "And he doesn't want the garage."

"I thought you said he wanted to buy—"

"Property. He wants the property." Jake's scarf-wrapped neck made an appearance, showing his increased bravery.

"Why would anyone want the property?" Stella asked.

He shrank back to cheek level. "Don't know. Don't care. It's a lot of money. Money I need."

Stella hopped down from the front steps into the dormant rose bed, crunching mulch below her. "We all need money, but we don't evict people to get it. Tell me who this person is. I'll talk to them."

"No way. Not gonna help you chase off the buyer."

Stella needed a plan. A way to get the information she needed to thwart this sale. "Give me some time, then. That's only fair."

Silence.

Good. That meant he was thinking about it. She channeled her best inner-Carissa and cleared her throat. "You know I've struggled to make this work, but I have a plan. I just need more time." She leaned her head against the damp, icy siding and willed her mood to remain calm.

"What plan?"

She pressed her finger to the frosted glass of a basement window and drew a car, thinking of her next words carefully. "You know I've struggled with all the new computer systems in the cars. I've decided to purchase a diagnostic computer so that I can work on all cars, not just classics." Her finger rubbed harder, causing a loud squeal from her leather gloves.

"You said you'd never give in to the, how did you put it... um... Oh right. You'd never give in to the snotty, glorified walking terminators that rich, lazy drivers are selling their souls to drive."

"Things change." She hated change, but no matter how hard she tried to hold on to the past, it slipped away every time. Ever since those discount corporate car places opened outside of town, she hadn't done well. Carissa, her best friend turned nauseatingly happy love bird, never had time for her anymore. Her grandparents who'd raised her had passed away, her father was in jail somewhere, and her mother... Well, who knew. In search of fame, she'd abandoned Stella when she was young and did her a solid, never returning—unlike her father. Apparently fame had eluded her, since Stella had never seen her on social media. A place she'd scoured for months after her *abuelo* passed. The man had always said Stella was the spitting image of her mother, with the attitude of her dear *abuela*.

"You could always move your garage. Then I could make money and you could still run your business."

"No!" she shouted and shot up straight. She paused to calm herself again, adjusting her leather jacket. The one Carissa had given her three Christmases ago. The girl was always thoughtful and giving and kind and now absent.

Great, so much for channeling her inner Carissa. Stella couldn't even control her temper for five minutes for the sake of her *abuelo's* garage. "Jake..." She swallowed the stomach-lurching boulder of pride and said a word she didn't even know was part of her vocabulary. "Please."

Begging. Is that what she was reduced to, all because no one had a love for classic cars anymore? The entire world was obsessed with the future and dismissed the past.

"You have thirty days to get the money, but I won't make you close shop until sixty days." Jake snatched the curtains shut, and Stella had no choice but to face the truth about her future.

She had to figure out how to get the money for the computer she needed. It looked like the only choice she had was to humble herself and play nice with Knox Brevard in order to drive business to her garage the way he'd done for Carissa with that stupid Internet show.

That was a huge price to pay. Humbling herself for some wannabe star like her bio mom and dad made her stomach swish and bubble and revolt. It wouldn't be easy, but it would be worth it to save her *abuelo's* shop. She owed him that. The only family that had ever believed in her, encouraged her, loved her.

THREE

Knox slumped over his mug, inhaling the magical concoction that one of the Fabulous Five, Mary Beth, had created. He inhaled the aroma of cardamom, the distinctive smell of mild spice, with a hint of nutty sweetness, a dash of woods. The unmistakable signature of an Iraqi coffee flooded him with emotions. How many times had he hoped for an offer to join Alima's family for coffee? The day that invitation finally came flashed like a lightning bolt charged by God himself.

He shoved the memory away before it rendered him breathless on the floor in the heart of the coffee shop. The horror of that day was too much to face in a public place where cameras could capture his meltdown. The desire to abandon his spot overwhelmed him. He gripped the ceramic mug so tight he thought it would shatter into tiny pieces. If he stood, he knew his legs wouldn't be strong enough to support him.

Despite his desire to flee from the memories, he was drawn to the coffee once more. He closed his eyes and imagined the good times, although sparse, and focused on one memory. Alima sitting across from him, explaining their coffee traditions. Her dark hair a stark contrast to the flowing silk scarf wrapped around her head and neck. The loose-fitting clothing had done nothing to hide her shape, not that he could ever steer his attention beyond her vibrant, dark-rimmed, long lash–framed eyes. The kind of eyes that had depth beyond her years and geographic experience.

Under the aroma of cardamom he discovered hints of other spices, as if Mary-Beth had managed to convince an Iraqi family to part with their coffee spice secret. Something that wasn't done.

He leaned over the mug, allowing the steam to caress his burning, windblown face. When he'd first arrived in town, he thought the gossip about Mary-Beth, the coffee whisperer, was a myth. Nope. It was true. The woman knew how to create the perfect beverage for any person.

His eyes watered, so he leaned away from the cup of memories, where he'd lost himself in another place, another world, another life.

When Drew and Lori had told him about Sugar Maple, he'd thought they'd been exaggerating, but it was really small-town America where everyone knew everyone else's business. Not too unlike the villages of Iraq.

For a few seconds, life didn't seem so bad. He hadn't felt the comradery of townspeople for a long time. The big city had allowed him that luxury. To remain in his own space without too much personal contact. Life was better that way.

Maybe doing more segments in this town wouldn't be such a bad idea. He'd definitely want to do one on the mystery of the coffee whisperer. It would be a tall order, though, to figure out how to capture Mary-Beth's gift.

This was the first time in as long as he could remember that he'd had the opportunity to complete a thought without a camera in his face or someone asking for his autograph. He savored the moment of peace until the front door opened, sending a gust of frigid air through the café. "Close the door already," he grumbled.

Click. Click. Click.

The unmistakable sound of Jacqueline Ramor's stilettos didn't send his pulse racing like he'd anticipated, but she'd be a welcomed distraction from his memories. Being the outcast of the Fabulous Five, nicknamed Judas Jackie, meant they shared in their misery. When first arriving, he was sure they'd hook up, but he didn't even aspire to have her on his arm for some big event. She was more like a sister to him now. An irritating, self-absorbed sister.

"Grump, much?" Jacqueline slid into the chair across from him and tapped the tip of her fire engine–colored nails to the tabletop. "Guess your mood tells me the answer to the question I came to ask."

He let go of the cup of distraction and lifted his head to see her eyelashes that extended to millimeters below her dark brows. "And that was?"

"If you'd be working with me on the next segment." She wrapped her long fingers around his mug and slid it toward herself, but he covered the rim with his hand, stopping the movement. Sharing wasn't his strongest character trait. Probably why relationships never were attractive to him, despite Lori's overanalyzing mumbo jumbo about him not wanting to lose anyone else in his life after losing so many brothers in war. If she ever found out about Alima, she'd never give him room to breathe.

"Do you want me to order you something?" Knox knew he'd have to tell Jacqueline the deal about the show and hoped one of Mary-Beth's mood-altering concoctions could distract her enough for her not to cause a scene.

Not that he was scared of Jacqueline, but there was a woman with her phone already out and eyeing him. The last thing he needed was a picture of a mug of coffee over his head going viral...again.

Jacqueline eyed the counter and then glanced back at him before relinquishing her hold. "No. I've got to go in a minute."

Before she had a chance to change her mind, he downed a gulp, sending warmth to his toes. It wasn't as bitter as an Iraqi coffee, but it still had the flavor. "You're right. We're not doing your segment next. I know you'd hoped for that, but we'd planned to do one full sweep of the town for the next segment and then move on."

"But that isn't the plan anymore." Jacqueline tapped her nails harder. "Word in town is that you're going to be doing several segments highlighting businesses. According to my sources, the segment on Carissa's shop put you back on top with your fans—and then some."

"That's true." He cradled the mug and took another long draw.

"Then you should focus on the one business in town that will take you to the next level. Let's face it... Coffee shops are everywhere." She pointed one finger toward the ceiling and then to the squealing espresso machine sending steam upward. She paused, but to his relief, it wasn't long enough to allow him to speak. "Then there's Felicia's Nursery—well, that's out, considering its winter and spring could be weeks away. That only leaves the grease pit." She giggled, but apparently he had to work on his poker face because her grin turned into an uncharacteristic nervous chuckle. "Wait, you're not serious. Sassy, sarcastic, scornful Stella is going to be your next poster girl for sweet, small-town Sugar Maple?" Her hands dropped to her lap. She sat upright, mouth open, eyes wide, looking like a petrified Jacqueline mummy.

"They've gotten to you. The elders, the small-town crazies... They brain-freezed you or something. I mean..." Her eyebrows reactivated like an animatronic and rose toward her hairline. "You of all people should appreciate what I can offer your show." She fluffed her hair and regained her composure. "Polished perfection. Isn't that what your viewers deserve? What they want and crave?" She placed her forearms on the table and slid closer to him, touching his hand with one of those nails. "Together, we could make your show number one."

Knox had never shied away from a flirt before, but there was a first for everything. Perhaps it was the fact he didn't feel like he had a choice. It took a second for his words to form, but he got there. "If this was my choice, it would be all about you, hon. I mean, look at you."

That provoked a bright-red-lip smile. "It's your show. Your choice."

"Unfortunately, it isn't. Not this time. Yes, I run my show, but the Internet world is capricious. My audience dictates what I do. Without their support, there is no show."

"Who told you your audience wants Stella? After what happened with your last automotive repair place...I mean..." She gripped his hand tighter. "I just want to see you become number one. Isn't that what you want? To be the best?"

"Yeah, I guess."

"You guess?" Jacqueline pulled away and pushed her chair out with a squeal. "I thought I had a winner here. Someone like myself. When you wake up and realize the colossal mistake you're making, give me a call." Her stilettos beat indentions into the old wood floor on her way out.

Great. He'd alienated the one person in this town he had anything in common with. A woman who understood why mediocre was never an option. Perhaps he'd invite her out for a nice meal to smooth things over and try to explain the situation better. He hated to eat alone in public.

Before he had a second to recover, Stella entered the coffee house with her Buick-sized attitude. She shuffled over in her military-style boots and halted with a squeal of leather to hard wood. "Listen, if you want this show, fine. I'll do it. I'll lower myself to the people-pleasing, accolade-craving, *need the world's superficial approval to feel worthy* show. Let's get it over with quick. I'll be ready first thing in the morning."

She about-faced on her scuffed size sixes and headed for the door.

"What if I don't want to work with a stubborn, underachieving, combative, sassy woman pretending not to care what other people think because she's too scared to face the truth?"

The boots screeched to a halt only a few steps from her grand exit. He had to give her credit... She had as much flair as Jacqueline but in an abrasive, impressive kind of way.

"Sassy?" She returned to the table. "You've been talking to your girlfriend."

"She's not my girlfriend."

"Whoa, no need to be hostile. Sounds like she already dumped you for the next eye-candy that strolled by. Or wait, did she find out I'm in and she's out? That must've been an explosive scene."

The eyes of the residents of Sugar Maple were homing in on him. How long would it be until someone posted a video of his two-time girl walk-out in minutes? That wouldn't help his image at all. He nudged the chair out with his foot. "Sit. I think we need to talk before either of us agrees to this."

She crossed her arms over her chest, and he was sure she'd bolt, but instead she flopped down into the chair. "Speak."

The woman in the corner slid her phone back into her jacket pocket, apparently deciding there wasn't going to be a show.

"First of all, this is not something you can start filming in the morning."

She opened her mouth, but he held up one hand. To his surprise, she didn't talk back to him. Maybe she wanted this but wouldn't admit it.

"If we move forward with this segment, I'll need to know everything about you. I refuse to move forward with a business that turns out to be—"

"Stealing from the innocent elderly?"

"You saw that segment?" he asked, the hair on the back of his neck matching her posture, rigid and straight.

"Don't flatter yourself. I don't watch your show." She shrugged. "I hear things."

He clasped his hands around the now lukewarm cup and took a break long enough to enjoy another sip.

"What did Mary-Beth make you? Some frou-frou caramel, green tea California concoction?"

He lowered the mug enough to see over the rim. "No, it's a blend of cardamom, cinnamon, and I think nutmeg."

She relaxed a little, as if his drink told her he wasn't such a bad guy. Her arms slipped down, her shoulders lowered from her ears, and an eyebrow quirked. "Never heard of cardamom. What is it?"

"It's a spice," he said with an air of superiority. Not because he wanted to put Stella in her place but because he found that always turned people away from asking more questions.

"Still don't know it," Stella said with a don't-care-what-you-think-of-me tone. Good for her. He could respect a woman who didn't try to be something she wasn't. "I don't like people digging into my business."

"It's part of the job. You share with me, I'll show your business to my viewers, and you can retire early with the patrons who will flock to your garage."

"Sure, I will." She rested her elbows on her legs. "Tell me why you want my business instead of Jacqueline's. It's obvious you already had a problem with a garage in the past and you don't want to work with me over Jacqueline, so why? It's your show, your rules, right?"

"It's difficult to explain, but I don't actually make the rules. My viewers and superfans are the ones who dictate content, and they can be fickle. One second they love me; the next I'm the most worthless human on this planet. I've had a good ride so far, but I want to take this to the next level. Move out of Internet and into streaming. It's the next logical step in my opinion."

"Doesn't sound so hard to explain. Makes sense." Stella let down her hair and strung the band around her wrist. The dark waves flowed around her cheeks and neck. To his surprise, they looked soft and beautiful. A juxtaposition to her abrasive nature.

"Why don't I take you to dinner tonight and we can discuss this further?" A meal with an intriguing, dark-haired, strong woman could be the most excitement he'd had since arriving in Sugar Maple.

She laughed.

He drifted his gaze to check the woman who had her camera in her hand once more. "What's so funny?"

"You taking me out on a date."

Since when did any woman not jump at that chance? "Business dinner," he said, but deep down, he did want to go out with her. He'd noticed her the first day he arrived, but then he and Jacqueline hit it off and Stella disappeared, except in passing on the street. He'd noticed her on more than one occasion if he was being honest with himself. He didn't want a relationship, or even to date, but dinner would be acceptable.

Stella's dark eyes sparkled like a kid on Halloween planning to play a trick instead of enjoying a treat. "I'm not cheap."

"Name the best place in town." Knox rested his heel on his other leg and watched the tough exterior of the proud Stella

Frayser crumble. "I'm sure we can come to some arrangement. Everyone has a price."

Her soft features hardened. "Thank you for stopping me from making a huge mistake. There has to be another way," she mumbled but loud enough for him to hear. She stood, looking down her nose at him. "I don't think you understand. I'm not like the other women you're used to dealing with. Dangling the promise of fame in front of me won't work. I'm not for sale."

FOUR

Stella had a difficult time concentrating, despite early morning hours usually being her best time of day. Darn if she hadn't wanted to go on that stupid date with Fame Hog. More likely, she just liked the idea of a date. How long had it been? For the briefest of moments, she'd allowed herself to envision a nice evening with an attractive man. And at this moment, she wished she had accepted, if for no other reason than to avoid a Fabulous Five intervention. "Girls' night?" Stella buttoned up her garage overalls. "You're insane. An awkward night of bonding between friends turned frenemies turned…whatever, doesn't sound good to me."

Felicia, the negotiator of their friend group, moved in with purpose. "If Carissa can forgive Jackie for stealing her fiancé from her a decade ago, certainly you can."

"Ha. Carissa's in an infatuation fog. She'd forgive the Grinch for stealing Christmas."

Felicia didn't sigh, argue, or reprimand. She did her mediator bit of listening, hearing, and reiterating what you already said. The girl was a saint. "I understand you want to protect

Carissa and the rest of us, but Jackie isn't trying to steal anything from anyone. She's learned her lesson."

"For now." Stella rolled up her overall sleeves and sat on the cold garage floor. "I know we agreed to a truce between all of us, and I don't actually mind seeing Jacqueline as much as I used to, but I'm not painting her nails or pretending we're still the Fabulous Five from high school."

"No one would expect that of you. I promise." Felicia handed Stella a wrench, as if it were the only tool she could possibly need to fix a car.

Stella shook her head and pointed to the socket wrench. Then she slid under her 1957 Chevy, ignoring Felicia's plea. The car needed more parts than she could afford. That's why she'd never been able to finish restoring it, something she dreamed of doing. But it was just one more unattainable life goal.

"I think Carissa might have a big announcement. Don't you want to be there? She's your best friend."

"Great. Wedding bells for my bestie and Dopey Drew." The words were bitter, but not because Stella hated the guy. He was good enough and made Carissa happy, but how could Stella like the man who stole her best friend, leaving her alone in the world? Again.

Felicia knelt by the front wheel and leaned down to look under the car. The girl was too pretty and too put-together to be on a garage floor. Stella tightened the exhaust bolts, hoping Felicia would take the hint. "You know you haven't lost her. She's remaining here in Sugar Maple. You can still see her all the time."

"Yeah, until she starts popping pups and stuff."

Felicia lay down on her side, as if she could force Stella to break her concentration. The girl had stunning, piercing blue eyes, a mesmerizing contrast to her dark hair. Stella had always thought the people who had teased Felicia for being from a black father and white mother were stupid or jealous. The girl wasn't just pretty; she was naturally beautiful and unique. "Don't be like that. You should be happy for your friend."

"I'm happy for her." Stella huffed, as if Felicia were intruding on her hours of work piling up on her. If only there was any truth to Stella having to work, she'd be in a much better mood. She slid out from under the car and stood, wiping her hands on a rag, hoping to stall long enough to find the right words.

Felicia studied the oil stain on the floor as if it was a psychological inkblot test. "I know you don't believe in happily ever afters. How could you, after your mother and father ran off and your father returned, only to steal everything, including your love."

Her words sent a rush of stinging fluid through Stella's veins. "Enough, Dr. Felicia. No head-shrinking me. I can't afford you."

Felicia smiled, her nonthreatening, I've-got-you warm smile that usually threw Stella off guard, but not today. "Then join us tonight. We'll have a great time." Felicia propped up on her elbow but didn't stand, as if she knew Stella would retreat back under the car at any moment.

Stella had to think fast. "I would, but I was invited to dinner." Lies. She never told them, but that one slipped out. It wasn't technically a lie, though. She had been invited to dinner. Felicia didn't need to know she'd turned Knox down. The man was too full of himself. He and Jackie were perfect for each other. No way he'd ever stick around a grease pit like this or her.

Felicia shot up from the ground and stood like a guppy out of water.

"Men do find me attractive, you know." Stella hated herself for actually considering the date. For the briefest of moments, she allowed herself to imagine the handsome, charismatic man who had drawn her attention the minute he'd sauntered into town being date worthy. Perhaps it was because she was date *deprived.*

Stella wiped down the socket wrench and set it on the chipped black counter. The one her father had hit with a sledge-hammer before telling her grandfather he was worthless and he was leaving. And on the way out, he'd looked over his shoulder and said, "And since you're such a great father figure, you can keep Stella." Those words stung as much today as they did all those years ago.

Felicia's mouth snapped shut. She flipped her hair over her shoulder and closed in on Stella as if to interrogate her until she cracked. "Who?"

Uh-oh. She was in trouble now. "What?"

"Who're you going to dinner with?" Felicia asked. Her shining, probing, scarier-than-a-nun's gaze probed for answers.

Stella tossed the rag down and bolted to the corner of the garage to her grandfather's six-foot-tall toolbox and rummaged for something. What, she didn't know. It didn't matter, as long as she didn't have to face Felicia another minute or she'd cave.

"Stella Frayser, do you have a date? I mean, with someone you like?"

"Is it really so impossible to imagine that someone would want to go out with me?" Stella opened and then closed a drawer and then opened another one.

"No, more like impossible that you would agree. You don't date."

"I've dated."

"When—2012?" Felicia's footsteps tapped up behind Stella, causing the hair on the back of her neck to stand at attention.

She needed to find a quick route out of this conversation before she crashed and burned. She forced a casualness to her voice. "I hope you guys have a great time. I'll catch you all on the next girls' night."

"No way. I'm not leaving until you spill the nuts and bolts." Felicia's foot tap, tap, tapped.

"Nuts and bolts?" Stella stood on the footstool and opened the top lid of the toolbox but dared a quick glance over her shoulder.

Felicia shrugged. "I'm trying to speak car."

Stella shook her head and analyzed the screwdrivers. "You need to study the vernacular better."

"Don't change the subject." Felicia moved in faster than a Lotus attacking a corner. "I'm not going to let you tell me a lie so that you can avoid girl's night. You can accuse me of anything you want, but I know you, Stella. You'll do whatever it takes to get out of spending the evening with Jacqueline and all of us because you think it'll be a waste of time. But I'm asking you to do this for Carissa. For me. Give our Fabulous Five another chance. Stop running away from those who care about you."

"I'm not a coward who runs from things. I told you, I can't," Stella said with a little less authority in her voice. Great. If she didn't figure out something in a minute, she'd be getting her hair braided by Judas Jackie in an hour. Felicia had a gift for convincing you to do the right thing, even if you didn't like it.

"Right, because you're going to dinner tonight. With whom?" Felicia's foot tapped again.

Stella closed the lid and climbed off the stepstool. "No. I'm not an open book for this town. You'll go blab to the rest of the girls."

Felicia's brows furrowed, and she tilted her head in that less than cordial way she did when she was really mad. "You know me better than that. If you really have dinner plans with some-one, you can tell me who. If you don't, then you're coming tonight." She crossed her arms and popped her hip out, taking the I'm-going-to-win-this-argument stance.

Stella felt like she was driving a car with bald tires on black ice. Like her *abuelo* had taught her, she analyzed all the options, but she'd run out of turns to take in this conversation.

"I'm afraid she can't." A deep, sultry, movie star voice echoed through the tall-ceilinged bay. "I asked Stella to dinner tonight. I apologize if I've ruined any of your plans." Knox Brevard strolled into the center of Stella's garage and saved her from a night of torture, but at what price? No, she wouldn't play this game.

"Listen, I—"

"No, I'm sorry. I should've believed you." Felicia backed away, running into the lift handle. She cringed and rubbed her back but recovered and shuffled toward the door. "I'll let the girls know that you had plans tonight. Don't worry, I get it now. I won't say a word."

"Wait. No. It's business. It's not a date."

Felicia disappeared with the door slamming shut behind her. Why hadn't Knox made a loud entrance like that? Then she would've been prepared to deal with him.

He walked up behind her and slung his arm over her shoulders. "She who doth protest too much..."

FIVE

There was a hint of spring in the air, as if to promise that this venture wouldn't be the epic fail Knox expected it to be. The woman didn't like him for whatever reason, and he needed to convince her to do this show if he wanted to work with a real television network. What was Drew thinking, making this deal?

He wasn't. Not since Carissa entered his life.

Perhaps if he spent some time with Stella, he'd figure out how to win her over. Not for himself but for the show.

He couldn't deny that the girl would film well for the segment. Not an obvious Jacqueline, sophisticated type, but Stella looked adorable in her overalls. Not beautiful like a girl he'd have on his arm for photo ops or his fans would think he'd lost his mind, but she definitely had a way about her that intrigued him.

Tonight, he needed to put on the charm to get her talking. That always worked. Once he knew more about her, he'd be able to figure out another angle. Perhaps something more sensational than an old, dirty garage.

He found himself in the center of town eyeing the various

businesses. None of them looked like a decent place to take Stella.

An older couple passed by with a southern greeting. He'd learned to wave back or it would be considered rude. Strange how people in the south felt the need to connect each time they saw one another. He snagged his phone and searched for nice restaurants near him. After scrolling through page after page and not finding anything useful, he decided a local would be a better source. The bakery still overflowed with people thanks to his show, and the café would be full of patrons, too. He needed to get to work on figuring out how to persuade Stella to do the show.

He spotted Davey, the town elder who had convinced Drew to tar and southernize himself to win Carissa over. How his friend was suckered into covering himself with maple syrup and posting notes on himself in front of the entire town was insane. All because of a crazy, made-up town legend. Nope, Davey wasn't the man for the job. He needed a woman's suggestion anyway.

Jacqueline's shop looked empty, and he needed to smooth things over with her. After all, she had helped him navigate around when he had first arrived. She was kind in her own way, and they understood each other.

But would she even let him in the door? The florist appeared open, so he made a quick stop and purchased some flowers and then sauntered over to Jacqueline's shop. To his surprise, there wasn't one patron inside.

He eyed the clothing: professional, flattering, vibrant colors. Why wasn't this place filled with customers?

"I'm not sure I have anything that'll fit you." Jacqueline abandoned the steamer near the back corner, where she was working on pressing a garment, and approached.

"Hi, there. I brought these for you. Beautiful flowers for a beautiful lady, not that they can compare." He winked.

She ate it up. The smile on her face told him he'd chosen well with the bright colors and oversize bouquet. This girl liked things to be flashy and noticed. He got her, making life easier around her. Why couldn't Stella fit that mold?

"Well, I guess I can let you in to the shop." She took the flowers and smelled them before heading to the counter in the back.

"These clothes are beautiful. The drawings don't do them justice. I know you don't believe me, but I tried to do your shop next."

"I know. Ms. Horton came by to explain what was going on. She did a pity buy to smooth things over, but I doubt she'll ever wear what she purchased." Jacqueline sighed. An unappreciated, failed business kind of sigh.

"That's because these women in this town don't know real fashion."

"Neither did New York." Jacqueline retrieved a large vase from a cabinet behind her and removed the green paper and plastic wrapping from the flowers, cut the stems, and arranged them in the glass vase so they were even more beautiful than before.

"I thought you chose to return here to mend some sort of old rift between you and the girls." Knox leaned over the counter, hoping to turn the conversation down memory lane to get some sort of lead.

"Yeah, well, that's partly true. Anyway, I'll figure something out. I always do," she said with a faux enthusiasm he saw through.

"I really am sorry."

She straightened and pushed her long, beautiful red hair

behind her shoulders. "I've got a plan; don't worry about me. I'm a winner, remember?"

"You are; I have no doubt." Knox patted her arm in that flirtatious way that always made her smile. "The girl who makes this town a little more sophisticated and a little brighter."

"Ditto." She crumpled the remnants of wrapping and placed it in the trash.

Knox eyed the merchandise in the store. "Hey, Lori's birthday is coming up. Would you do me a favor and pick something out for me and send it to her? But, ah, tell her I picked it out." He chuckled. "For some reason, she always gets upset when I tell her to go buy herself something for her birthday. She says I need to pick it out." He shrugged. "I don't get it, because if I did she'd return whatever I chose."

"Women like to believe a man knows them well enough to pick out the perfect gift. That being said, I prefer to avoid the drama and pick it out myself." She rounded the counter and hip bumped him. "So are you going to tell me why you're really here? Let me guess... You need help dealing with Stella."

"Actually, now that you mention it. I just need a restaurant to take her to so that we can come up with a plan. I need a nice place that will catch her off guard so that I can get her talking. If I'm going to convince her to do the show, I need more information. It's the only way I can continue working to help the town and your businesses." His words were empty, but Jacqueline needed hope right now, not the bitter truth. He'd already given that to her, and she didn't want it.

"Is that all? Sure, I can help you with that," she said, her voice rising to the overly friendly tone. "You know she's all wrong for you, though, right?"

He chuckled, relieved Drew wasn't around to call him out for his nervous habit. "I'm interested in a business relationship only."

"Right. You're not looking for anything serious in your life. Yep, I remember."

He opened his mouth to say something but decided it would be best to let that comment slide since he didn't want to get into a deep discussion right now.

She studied her red nails. "There's a great date place only a few blocks from town."

"It's not a date." He slid his hand into the crook of her arm and leaned into her. "I know this isn't fair. Listen, I respect you and I want to help. Even if it isn't with the show right now, let's get together and chat about ways we can help each other. Next week I'll take you out for a nice dinner. How does that sound?"

She didn't respond to his offer. Instead, she slipped from his reach and returned to steaming the dress in the corner of her shop. "Lester's. It's a steak place. She'll love it. Red tablecloths and twinkling candlelight. You'll woo her into your clutches in no time."

"I don't want to clutch her. As you said, she's not like us." Knox offered a parting smile that he knew would soften Jacqueline and then headed for the door.

"You're right. She's too good for us."

He ignored Jacqueline's parting words since he knew her tactics of trying to bait him with one thing and then draw him into a conversation about herself. The woman was manipulative when she wanted something, and she wanted him. Not in a romantic way but as a man to give her a chance at being famous.

Stella was the opposite of them, but that didn't make her better. She was abrasive but intriguing. Tonight, he'd wine and dine her and figure out what made Stella Frayser tick. By tomorrow, he'd have her bending to his will. If there was one thing he knew in life, it was winning a woman over. Stella was different than his normal breed but still a woman.

SIX

Stella wiped her hands and checked the price on the car diagnostic computer. It hadn't changed since the last time she'd checked. It didn't matter if it was two dollars or two million. She couldn't afford it right now.

She eyed the 1957 Chevy she'd been restoring forever and knew her plans would be put on hold yet again. There went her promise to her *abuelo* once again to fully restore his beloved car. If she didn't have to buy vintage parts, she could have it done already, but that would make her *abuelo* roll over in his grave.

Nope, it had to be done right. And if she didn't want to sell her soul to the Internet sensation, she'd have to find a way to buy the diagnostic computer and suck it up fixing the mind-numbing fancy cars of today. She typed a quick email to the garage owner that had offered his computer secondhand to her, letting him know she wanted to buy it. How, she didn't know, but she'd figure out some way to come up with the money.

She'd already tried social media, but she couldn't compete with the chain shops outside of town, especially when they could do twice the work in half the time. Even if they didn't do it well. She'd already tried refurbishing old cars, but no one in town cared about classics. She'd already tried to post fliers, create online advertisements, and more, but only a drizzle of customers had come and she needed a deluge.

"Hey, you open?" Jackie's voice pierced the tranquil moaning sounds of Stella's old garage space heater near her desk.

"Not for your car. Not yet at least." She hit the lock button on her computer and hopped off the stool. "What do you want?"

"Direct as always, I see." Jackie crossed the garage floor with the tapping of her heels against the cement. She draped a garment bag over the chair and set a shoe box on her desk. "I brought you something for your hot date tonight."

"Felicia told you? That traitor. Last time I'm going to trust her." Stella rubbed at her fingers, trying to dislodge the grime from the bed of her nails until she could stumble over an explanation. "It's not a date. You've been misinformed."

"Felicia didn't tell me."

Stella blinked at her and then narrowed her eyes. "What game are you playing?"

"Knox came by to let me know." Jackie unzipped the garment bag. "After he told me about your date—"

"Not a date." At least not a real one, something she kept telling herself.

"Your evening out," Jackie said with a smile that looked as sweet as a Carissa greeting, but Stella knew better. That expression was covering a devious plan. "I knew I had to help." Jackie slid a white, form-fitting, *Paris runway* dress from the bag and held it up to Stella.

"I'm not wearing that."

"Don't be silly. You don't have anything but pants, combat boots, and a leather jacket. That isn't non-date attire."

"It's not me. And this is a business dinner. Nothing more." Stella backed away from the doll dress and rounded the desk to block Jackie's fashion makeover. She wanted to go out, but not in Jackie style.

"Right. Then if you're in this for your business, you need to play the game. The way to play the game is to distract Knox from what he wants so you can get what you want." Jackie held the dress out to her. "Do you want to save your shop or not?"

Stella's hand grasped the dress, but her gut was twisting with warning. No way she'd wear it, but perhaps the shoes would be something worth taking a look at. She could compromise and wear a nice shirt and shoes. "I don't want to play games like you, Jackie. That isn't me. If Knox wants to work with me, then he needs to accept me for who I am. If not, then I wouldn't want to work with him." Or anything else with him.

"Not even to save your grandfather's garage?"

A sharp pain shot through Stella's chest. She'd do anything in the memory of her *abuelo*, but this? Dressing herself up like a doll and parading around like a...a Jacqueline replica wasn't an option. "I'm going to save my shop."

"How?" Jackie set the dress on the back of the chair and rounded the desk.

"I'm going to buy a computer to work on newer, computerized cars."

"You hate anything that isn't older than our parents. You've never wanted anything newer than early 1970s."

"Things change. I'm willing to open my garage to yuppies like you in order to make enough to keep this garage going."

"So you have the money for the computer?" Jackie asked. "Town gossip mill says you have sixty days to turn this place around."

Stella noticed her boots were covered in dirt. She'd clean them before tonight. That was making some sort of effort. "No, but I'll just have to tighten my belt."

"Tighten it any more, and it'll make your waist smaller than a corset would." Jackie paced from Stella's desk to the Chevy and back. "Listen, you're right. You shouldn't have to dress up and flirt to win over Knox, but it is what it is. Maybe you can tell him you want to be paid. He seems to be pretty sure that this is the segment he wants to do. Make him work for it. You need to distract him with your pretty figure and then tell him what you want. It works. Trust me."

"I'm not you," Stella said with an air of disgust. "I don't mean that you're not, um... Heck, you're you and I'm me. I'm not good at fashion and guys. You are. I'll go tonight, tell him that I need the money, and see what he says."

Jackie shook her head and sighed. "Oh, my poor Stella. You still believe that what happens in the world is fair."

"Are you seriously saying that to me? The girl who was abandoned by both parents and dealt with a father being arrested that everyone in town knew about? Did you forget the teasing I endured and how many parties I was excluded from in middle school because parents didn't want their kids hanging out with a con's daughter? Your parents?"

"I'm not my parents," Jackie snapped, her perfect façade cracked.

"Listen. I think I know the score on life. That doesn't mean I need to pretend to be someone I'm not. I can't do it. I won't. He either likes me for who I am, or he doesn't."

"For the show, you mean?" Jackie's eyebrow rose.

Stella blinked, opened her mouth, shut it, and then opened it again. "Yes, of course."

Jackie's expression went from tight-lipped and guarded to soft-eyed acceptance. "You're right. You should be you. If he doesn't accept you for who you are, then you're not the right person for his show."

A gleam of hope shone in Jackie's eyes. "I'll leave the dress here in case you want it. If not, you can pass it on to one of the other girls." She slid her purse up her arm and walked out of the building like it was a runway fashion show. The woman knew how to work a room.

Stella locked up the garage early, not concerned that anyone would come by who needed a repair anyway. If only her *abuelo* were here, he'd know what to do. He always seemed to keep this place going. Of course, the cars were different back then.

She went to her computer to shut it down when she noticed a reply from the shop owner with the computer.

Another offer came in, but I told him I'd check with you. Get me the money by the end of the day tomorrow and it's yours. If not, then I'm selling it to the other buyer.

Stella collapsed into her chair. This was her only shot of getting a decent computer. She couldn't pass up the opportunity, but her credit cards were maxed and she didn't have enough cash to buy it.

The white dress lay there as if mocking her resolve. How bad could it be to dress up and smile at a man? Her stomach churned at the thought, but the torn and crumpled eviction notice on her desk hammered at her resolve.

This would be a desperate act by a desperate person, but what other option did she have? Let go of the only thing she had left in this world, or sacrifice her pride. If Knox Brevard wanted a woman who dressed up, spoke softly, and smiled a lot— someone completely not...herself...

She could do that.

Maybe.

SEVEN

Knox finished answering fan email on his phone and then dialed Drew. The phone rang over the car speaker three times, and Knox cursed under his breath at the once-best-friend turned sap. By ring four, Knox glanced out the car window, but nothing was going on outside the tree-lined side street where the inn resided. He'd never seen so little activity in his life.

"Hey, what's up?" Drew answered on ring five with a lightness to his voice, as if they weren't working on the biggest deal of their lives. The deal that would free them both from the Internet world.

"If you don't have time to work because you're too busy helping your girlfriend, then send me the contact info for this mystery producer. I'll speak with him myself." Knox didn't even feel bad at the harshness of his tone.

"No need. He'll be here tomorrow afternoon. He wants to meet at Stella's garage." Drew mumbled something to Carissa in the background. Couldn't the guy pay attention for five seconds without interruption?

"The garage? Seriously?" Knox tossed his cell phone onto the passenger seat and headed through town.

"He insisted." Drew cleared his throat. "I've got to run. Carissa has to head out, and I'd like to walk her over to Felicia's house for some sort of get-together. I'll head to the inn after so we can talk about a game plan for tomorrow."

"I'll be out." Knox turned off of the main square and headed up the hill. "I have a meeting with Stella. I'll catch up with you after. Probably about an hour or an hour and a half."

"You're meeting with Stella?" Drew asked with a weighted tone.

Not in the mood to listen to someone else tell him he wasn't good enough for Stella, he reached for the End button on the console. "I'll see you in an hour." He pressed the button and pulled into the gravel lot. The rocks crunched under his wheels. The old-fashioned steel-siding building with an oversize garage door didn't look inviting enough to film. It looked like something on a 1960s horror film. But Knox didn't build his brand and Internet empire by giving up easily. He'd figure this out.

He got out of the car, slid his phone into his pants pocket, buttoned one button on his blazer, and strutted up the three rickety old steps to the glass door at the side of the garage.

A woman walked across the cement floor with long dark hair in a stark white dress. Now *that* was a woman he could see on his arm. The beautiful, hourglass shape looked unique, but when his gaze reached her face, he stumbled back off the top step.

His vision had to be playing tricks on him. That woman looked like Stella but different. Like a beautiful twin sister different. A put-together, jaw-dropping, car-stopping, naturally beautiful sister. His pulse double-timed.

The door lock clicked, nudging him to recover his composure. He switched on the charm in an instant. "Good evening."

"Hi, Knox. Give me a minute." The woman's voice sounded like Stella. Her arms still moved in a mechanical way like Stella's. She walked away, her ankles wobbling in the heels, but she managed to cross the room to a desk and return without tumbling over.

He cleared his throat, forcing words to come to the surface. *Get it together, man. You're Knox Brevard. Internet sensation. Ex-military.* "I could've picked you up at your house after work. I didn't mean to rush you."

"I live here."

He looked around and spotted a loft at the end of the garage. "You're not serious."

She did a biker-chick shrug. "I used to have a place in town, but it was a waste of money when I spend most of my time here anyway."

"What about carbon monoxide?"

Stella brushed past him into the gravel parking lot. "Not a problem. Let's go."

That was the woman he'd met before, direct and short with conversation. He raced ahead to open her door for her, but when her ankle rolled on the rocks, he grabbed her arm to keep her upright.

A slight gasp shot from her lips, so he stood her up and let go. "Sorry. Reflex."

"That's right, you're the hero type." She tucked her long hair behind her ear and stepped cautiously the few more feet to his car.

"You say that as if it's a bad thing."

"No, I just don't need a hero." She cleared her throat. "I mean, it's nice of you to take me to dinner to discuss business. Thank you."

That was the nicest and longest she'd spoken to him so far. Maybe there were more layers to this woman than he'd thought. Interesting... He could usually analyze, evaluate, and make a plan of action on a date by the time they reached the car. He needed to focus.

She gracefully slid into the leather seat and pulled her legs into the car. He still couldn't reconcile the frizzy-haired, abrasive girl in overalls with this woman. Intrigued, he raced around the car to his own seat and revved the engine, but it only clicked rapidly and didn't turn over.

Heat flamed his ears. Luckily she didn't know him well enough to see his tell like his military brothers always ragged on him about. Bozo Ears, they liked to call him back in the day. Never in front of the women, though. The men knew better than that. He missed the camaraderie of his men. The safety of their friendship. A man knew where he stood in a room full of soldiers and friends. "It's a rental."

She flicked on the light as if it would start the car, studied it, and then turned it back off. "Don't worry about it. I'll take a look." She flung open her door. "Pop the hood."

"What are you doing?" Knox jumped out of the driver's seat.

"I'm fixing your car. That's what I do." Stella looked at him with wide eyes and mouth ajar, like he wasn't following her words. He was following them, but they didn't compute. A woman who looked like that didn't get greasy and dirty working on cars.

"It's probably a bad battery. I'll call the rental company." He slid his phone out of his pocket, but she walked around him and popped the hood. "Only if you want to wait hours or ride my bike to dinner."

He dialed the number, but it rang and rang until it went to voice mail. "No answer."

"It's after hours." She jiggled and wiggled a few things under the hood, and he felt his man card melting in his pocket.

"I'll call Drew or Lori. They'll lend me their vehicle."

"No need." She pulled off one of her heels and banged it against the battery. "Try it now."

"Seriously?" Knox stood there looking at her but didn't move.

She waved her shoe around. "I'd prefer my work boots, but I guess there's still some power in a stiletto. That's what Jackie tells me, anyway."

A car went by on the street, but he didn't even look to see who passed. He couldn't tear his eyes away from this crazy, breathtaking, sassy woman who had grease on her hands and was dressed in high fashion.

"We can stand here all night or you can trust me."

"Trust you?" Those two words gutted him. The last woman to say that to him had been Alima. He had to move away before Stella saw the pain in his eyes he knew he could never hide. His legs threatened to buckle, so he collapsed into the driver's seat. With a little more forced energy, he pressed his foot to the brake and turned the key. To his amazement, the car roared to life.

A much-needed distraction to bring him back to the present.

He hid his old wounds behind his perfect smile and hopped out of the car. "You're amazing, Stiletto Stella."

"Great, we're on a nickname basis now and we haven't even reached appetizers." Stella closed the hood and wiped her palms together, smearing the little bit of grease.

"I'll wash up at the restaurant. Let's go. I've gotta be up early to take care of something." Stella settled into her seat, careful not to wipe the dirt onto her dress.

Knox didn't argue with her, not when he wanted to move this night along as much as she did. He needed to pick up his game if he wanted to charm this woman into submission for his project. No problem. He'd never met a woman he couldn't outmaneuver. He'd win her over by the main course. "You know, I think I have you figured out a little better. We're not too different, you know."

"No. Not any more different than a 1970 Dodge Charger to a new Tesla."

It took him a minute, but he figured out her metaphor. This girl wasn't just beautiful and a little intriguing, she was smart, too. "Yes, but they're both cars."

"We are all humans." She gave him a heart-stopping wink. He hadn't met a girl as exotic as Stella since, well, Alima. He gripped the steering wheel and willed himself to drive out of the gravel parking lot and through town away from his wayward thoughts.

"All I'm saying is that I think we can work together. I get that you're not interested in the show, but you want to save your garage. Am I right so far?"

"Yes..." she said with trepidation.

"And you enjoy working on cars."

"That doesn't take a genius to figure out. I own a garage." Stella took a chest-expanding breath that distracted him enough that he ran off the road and had to recover.

"Keep your eyes where they belong. I'm not one of your floozies you want to show off for your image." Stella eyed the road outside as if the passing grass was more interesting than his small talk.

The town shops were closed, but he caught a glance of Carissa and Drew walking down the street. Stella shrank down in her seat, telling him she didn't want to be seen with him, but why?

"I'm not looking for a woman to show off on my arm right now. Actually, I want to improve my reputation. Believe it or not, I'm not the womanizing Internet personality everyone thinks I am. I didn't bring you out to show you off and then drop you back home. I made an effort to figure you out better to take you to a place you wanted to go for dinner so you could enjoy a nice evening while we spoke about business. I didn't ask my receptionist to make the reservation. I didn't have a driver pick you up and have you meet me there. I made the reservation, I did the research, and I believe that you'll have a lovely evening because I put extra effort into making you feel special."

He turned off the main road and headed down a side street, spotting the red sign ahead for the restaurant.

"Why?" she asked.

"Why what?"

"Why are you trying to make me feel special?"

He thought about it for a moment and knew his normal schmoozing wouldn't work. "Because I was intrigued by you, which means you're special."

"I see." She studied the grease on her hands. "Tell me... All this research you did for the perfect date. Do you think it was worth it?"

He pulled into the parking lot, and it appeared to be a nice building with romantic twinkling lights with the aroma of hearty beef and garlic that wafted through the air vents. "Yes, this will be a great place for us to enjoy a good meal together."

"This five-star steak place?" she asked with a sweet smile.

"Yes. See, I do know what you like. I asked around."

Her smile turned into a grin that twisted a little further on one side than the other. "Yep, you know me so well." She opened the car door. "By the way, I'm a vegetarian."

EIGHT

Stella chastised herself silently. *What happened to being gracious and sweet?* Her defensiveness was going to ruin everything.

"I didn't know. I'm sorry. We'll go somewhere else." Knox appeared genuinely disappointed, which made her feel even worse. Yes, the guy was full of himself and superficial with no real substance, but she didn't have to be rude.

"No. It's fine. I'm sure they have salad or something."

He laughed, a bent-over-holding-his-gut laugh.

"What's so funny?" Her irritation grew, so she reminded herself she was trying to get the man to pay her ahead of time for her hours on the show.

"Sorry. It's just that—" he gasped "—the leather-wearing, car-fixing, biker woman is vegetarian."

"Faux leather."

He bent over the steering wheel, laughing harder and swiping at the tears in his eyes.

"Glad I could provide some entertainment for you." She got out of the car and marched to the front awning. For a celebrity type, he was fast, reaching the door before she could open it.

He held it shut. "Seriously, I'm not taking a vegetarian into a steakhouse." Knox stepped into her personal space. "I get it. You're right."

"About what?" Stella couldn't keep up with him. The man was all over the place.

"I don't know you. But Stiletto, I sure want to understand you better. I mean, you've got layers. It's been a long time since I met anyone I didn't figure out in the first thirty seconds of meeting them." He brushed his thumb over her knuckles, and she didn't like the way it left her body wanting his touch. "Name the place. I'll take you anywhere."

All she knew was this man needed to take a step back, and she could see he wasn't used to not getting his way all the time. "Fine, but if you're serious, then you get the real me. Not this made-up, sweet-talking girl who wants to win you over. It isn't working."

"This has been you sweet-talking me?" His brow arched in what Stella couldn't deny as a charismatic, stomach-stirring way.

"Yes. Maybe Jackie was right and you couldn't handle the real me."

His brow dropped, as did his smile. "Jacqueline, huh?"

She nodded, but before Knox said another word, Stella could already see that woman had done something more than lend her a dress.

"The same Jacqueline who told me to bring you to the best steakhouse in town?" He took a step back, allowing her to breathe in the too-tight dress before the stiches burst.

"I should've known." Stella rolled her eyes and stepped around the car. "This had Judas Jackie written all over it. She's so worried she's going to lose to me, she'll do anything to sabotage it. I can't believe I listened to her. Get in the car."

"Where are we going?" he asked but followed her lead, returning to his driver's side.

"Let's drop the pretense and figure out if we can work together or not. If not, then we move on. If so, then we move forward. We both want it to work for different reasons, so let's just speak frankly, iron out the details, and stop all these games." She wanted him to stop the tilt-a-whirl of emotions he evoked. The tight breath, irritating, soft touch, with a splattering of intrigue.

"Games?" he asked, as if offended by her words.

She put on her seat belt. "Games. Your entire life is a game, and I don't want to play. Here's how it's going to be. We'll discuss how we want the show to go and see if we can work this out. For now, drive."

"To where?" He started the car without argument, but she knew he wouldn't like her idea of what a good evening would be. Not a night of faux dating with expensive dinner and flirtatious touches. Instead, they'd have more of a garage-running, simple meeting with no pretense far from the limelight he so craved. "Go back to Main and then out the other side, up the hill, and then right."

"Okay. I like a woman who takes charge."

"No games, remember? You're not here to win me over with your attempt at charming me or playing hero." She had never and would never be manipulated by a man to get what they want. Her father had done it to her for too many years until he landed in jail. "Talk, eat, plan. That's the deal."

He held up one hand in surrender. "Okay, but I think you have the wrong opinion of me. You only know my brand, not me." His words sounded hoarse, as if there was more behind his statement than just small talk.

When they passed Mary-Beth's place and she saw the lights on, for a minute, she wished she wasn't missing out. Then she saw Jackie's car and remembered why they were no longer friends. The fiancé-of-her-best-friend-stealer wasn't her friend. Sure, she'd agreed to a cease fire, but that didn't mean she had to like the girl. And then this dress-bait, soaked in lies, chased with the realization that Stella didn't belong in Knox's world only made Stella resent Jackie more. "Do me one more favor?"

"What's that?"

"I know you and Jackie are a thing, but don't bring me into it. Don't ask her about me. Don't even talk to her about me. Got it?"

"Considering the advice I received last time, I think you're safe. For the record, though, Jackie and I are just friends. We understand each other and how we want success in our lives, but there's no chemistry between us."

Stella's pulse rate went over fifty-five, but she closed her eyes and willed away that foreign thought of possibility with a man like Knox Brevard with his womanizing and drinking and partying and his love only for money and fame.

The car turned down the street to Pedro's food truck. They had her favorite burritos in town and it was the one place she knew Knox would never eat...and Jackie would faint if she saw them there.

"Pedro's. Great. I've been wanting to try this. Lori told me it was good. I love bean burritos."

"You do?" Stella gave him the don't-lie-to-me side-stare.

Knox turned into a space and put the car in park. "Now who's making assumptions about people? You know, I'm not all stiff suits and applause seeking. I'm still a man who likes the simpler things in life."

There it was again, that undertone of sadness. It intrigued and drew her in, but she fought and managed to free herself from asking.

"It's been a while since I slowed down. Life is easier that way sometimes." He opened his door.

Let him go. Don't ask. You don't want to know anything about him except how to get this show over with.

He rounded the car and took Stella by her hand to escort her to the food truck.

"What do you mean it's easier sometimes to not slow down?"

He halted only two feet from the salvation of ordering their food. Her breath caught at the sight of his jaw twitching, his bicep straining against his jacket, and his eyes downcast and misty. "Not first-date conversation."

Date? First? She wanted to argue and tell him he was wrong. This wasn't a date, and if it was, it would be their last. But she couldn't. Not when the superficial, attention-seeking, wanna-be-hero-to-everyone Knox Brevard had shattered in front of her eyes and she found a glimpse of a wounded, vulnerable man underneath.

NINE

The spicy burrito left Knox's eyes watering and the back of his neck and forehead sweating. He dabbed at his face with a napkin while eyeing the garage from his lawn chair near an old large Chevy.

"Too much for you, city boy?" Stella said with a little kick of a Latino accent. A touch of sour cream creased the corner of her lips. He wanted to use it as an excuse to lean into her, but she'd probably slug him. She wasn't a girl he could move in on, unless he wanted his body to be found under a car. Alima had been brave for a woman in her position in life, but she'd never possessed the spunk Stella showed. After all, how could a woman in the Middle East with no real rights act in such a way? Alima had had great inner strength, though. Any woman with enough courage to introduce an American soldier to her family was strong. Who knew it would cost her her life?

He took another large bite, allowing the heat to sizzle on his tongue, down his throat, and into his stomach. He'd regret this later, but for now, it kept him grounded to this world and not slipping into the old one. "The car. Is it yours, or are you working on it for someone?"

"The Chevy was my *abuelo's*. I'd planned to fix it up and get it running, but something seems to always thwart my plans. I'll get her done someday, though. It's something we worked on together. It was the first car I ever tinkered with." Her gaze traveled over the car and obviously fond memories.

"You were close to your grandfather?"

"He and my *abuela* were everything to me. They raised me. My *abuela* was from Columbia and taught me how to cook and dream. My *abuelo* was from New York and taught me cars and bravery."

"And your parents?"

"No," she said flatly. "My turn."

He shifted in the lawn chair, the metal frame crying under his weight. "I promise to answer your questions, but for now, I need to know that I'm entering into a segment here that will work for my show. That you don't have any skeletons under your hood."

Stella placed her burrito on the wrapper in her lap and removed that dot of sour cream from her lips. "You said you want to get to know me in order to frame this series around me. Well, that street isn't one way. You're ex-military like Drew, right?"

He swallowed the dryness and took a long sip of soda through the tiny red straw. "Yep, we served together."

"How'd you go from ex-military to Internet sap?" Stella sighed. "I don't mean to sound rude. It's just that I can't reconcile the two. Combat missions to frivolous playtime."

The oversized clock on the wall clicked away like a timebomb. He took another long drink and settled his nerves. "Change. When you face such destruction, pain, loss... Frivolous is a vacation from that world."

She leaned toward him with soft eyes. "I guess I can understand that. Maybe you're not such a horrible person after all.

You know, if I strip away the arrogance, self-entitled parts and restore you to a pre-fame Knox."

The way she looked at him, as if she thought he was more than a womanizing personality, made him uneasy. He cleared his throat and set his drink on the floor. "Don't kid yourself. I'm who I am."

"A guy who hides his pain behind an image," Stella said in the softest tone he'd heard out of her so far. He didn't like it. Pity didn't work for him. It was part of the reason he'd never told Drew and Lori about Alima. Drew's squad had transferred out of the area before Knox had fallen in love with Alima, so Drew couldn't have known for sure if any of the stories were true. Sure, they'd heard rumors, but they never spoke about it. Knox would never speak about it again with anyone.

"My turn. What about your parents?" Maybe he could spin an HEA out of this garage story and earn some brownie points with his followers, ultimately securing his streaming show. That's why he was here.

"Gone. I'm the small-town cliché. Girl wasn't loved enough for her parents to choose her over drugs, fame, and crime. Mother ran off to pursue her dreams and never returned. Father ran off, only to return and end up in jail. Guess that ends this conversation."

"Did you do anything? Criminal, I mean? If so, tell me now. If not, I can still make this work."

"No. I'm poor. That doesn't make me a crook."

"If you need money to keep this place going, I can lend it to you."

"You're not playing my hero, and I'll never be indebted to a man." She took a bite of burrito that dripped refried beans onto her dress.

Knox grabbed his napkin and scooted closer to help, but the

way her jaw twitched told him to stand down, so he backed away. "You better go put that in cold water or it'll stain."

"No worries. It's not mine. Jackie dressed me up like a doll so I could embarrass myself trying to be someone I'm not." She smeared the refried bean stain across the material. "Serves her right."

"You know, that dress might have been meant to embarrass you, but it backfired."

A perfectly arched brow that framed her faux-leather-colored eyes raised at him.

"All I'm saying is that if I were you, I'd get that stain out and keep the dress, because you're more stunning than Jackie could ever pull off in any of her designs."

Stella narrowed her gaze and shook her head with a Buick-sized attitude on her shoulder. "I thought you weren't going to play games anymore."

He rolled up the remaining quarter of his burrito into the silver wrapping and set it by his drink. "I'm being honest. I thought you liked people to tell you things straight. Perhaps you hiding behind oversized garage overalls and grease stains is your way of protecting yourself. If you look unapproachable, then people will leave you alone."

"Okay, my turn, Dr. Brevard," she said. She took her last bite of burrito, and he couldn't imagine how a woman with her figure could eat like that. It was refreshing. He never liked the bony girls who never ate, but they had photographed well and they'd always managed to move on once he'd introduced them to the public. It was a win-win for everyone. "Maybe you're not the superficial, attention-seeking hog that everyone thinks you are. Perhaps you're hiding behind a brand to keep from letting people get to know the real Knox Brevard, if that's even your real name."

"What would I have to be hiding from?" He laughed, but he

heard the edge, despite his attempt to play off her accusations. The clock clicked away again, and he shot up. "I didn't realize it was getting so late. I promised Drew I'd meet up with him about tomorrow. You sure there's nothing about you I need to know before we move any further into this segment?"

"Nope. I'm good."

"I should go." He stood, but before he could take one step, she was in his face, a breath away.

"No. Not happening. You head-shrunk me. My turn." She stood eye-to-chin with him, but he didn't retreat.

"Tell me. You said something earlier about sometimes it being easier not to slow down."

He couldn't swallow, couldn't speak, couldn't breathe.

Images of a silk scarf flittering in the wind outside the blast zone came in like a nail gun to his skull. The pain pounded his head with unrelenting hammering until he closed his eyes and rubbed his temple.

A soft hand touched his wrist like a damp cloth to a fever—a barbaric fever that festered and invaded every part of him. It took several ticks of that damn clock on the wall before he managed to take in a stuttered breath. He released his head and blinked until the blurriness subsided. After another deep inhale, he opened his mouth, but she covered his lips with her fingers.

"No." She moved her hands to her side and stepped away.

His head swirled with too many thoughts to grasp any single coherent word.

"There are some things that are too painful to say aloud." She looked at her bare feet and the heels tossed to the side. "You're right. This isn't first-date conversation."

TEN

The mountain night air penetrated Knox's jacket, nipping at his skin like sand flies in the pit. The stinging, irritating feeling snaked into his resolve to forget all that he'd left behind in war. Somehow, Stella had brought it all to the surface again. Yet, when she'd touched his wrist, it was as if she'd grounded him enough to face what he'd tried so hard to forget.

He bent over the hood of the car in the back lot of the inn and breathed through the onslaught of memories. Thoughts swirled in his mind like a corkscrew, but he managed to keep his breath calm. For the first time since returning stateside, he allowed himself to see that day.

Hot air rippled over the boulders and buildings in the distance. The odor of diesel from the Hummers left an oily taste in his mouth. Heat of the midday sun, the unseen enemy to the men, seared the ground to a boot-melting temperature.

Another inhale of crisp, country air kept him from shaking, from running, from screaming. He recalled Stella's touch once more and forged on into forgotten territory he'd spent so much time avoiding.

The front door opened. Alima stepped out. No welcoming

kiss or holding of hands. No one could see their love in public, but he yearned to take her into his arms.

She smiled and tugged her scarf around her face. He was thankful she didn't have to be in a full burka all the time like some women.

His pulse raced and he glanced at his men around the Humvee. No one said anything, but they all knew he'd fallen for the wrong girl. He wasn't the first, nor would he be the last to succumb to such a fate during intense times. A little compassion when far from home went a long way to a man's heart. He didn't want to care for her, but she'd been sneaking him supplies and looking after him and his men. They'd steal a few moments together during each delivery. After a month or two, they were in love. Six months later, he knew it was time to make arrangements, to find a way to get her family to accept him, and then he'd be able to figure out how to get her out of the pit.

He'd been young, foolish, and naïve back then. The boy barely of age to balance the RPG long enough to fire before falling over.

The event that changed him forever fluttered to the surface.

The swoosh.

The explosion.

The silk scarf twisting in the wind.

He tried to push beyond the same spot his memory stopped at each time. But he couldn't see the rubble or the aftermath of the explosion. Even in his dreams, it always stopped with the scarf.

"I thought you were going to be an hour, hour and a half, tops?" Drew's voice shattered Knox's concentration. "What's wrong?" The sound of hiking boots on gravel crunched closer, so Knox stood tall and locked up the compartment of memories.

"Yeah, turns out Judas Jackie, as the girls call her, pulled a fast one on me, so it took a little longer than I thought to win

Stella over." He locked the car and marched past Drew. "We can go over stuff now, though."

"Sure. After you tell me what you were remembering a minute ago."

"What?" He kept walking. No way he was stopping for that convo. "Hey, I'm gonna go to my room first. That burrito is like a brick in my belly. This belt needs to be tossed for the night. I'll meet you in the parlor, or we can head to the office if you prefer."

"Parlor's fine. That way you and I can have a little chat." Drew jogged to catch up by the time Knox reached the front porch.

"Yeah, we can. I want to know what the deal is for tomorrow. That garage is nothing to look at, but we might be able to spin this into a Cinderella story."

Drew grabbed the screen door handle before Knox could get it. "Not gonna tell me what flashback hit you?"

"Flashback? Come on. No baggage here, dude. I left all that trash back in the pit. I'm here to have a good time, now."

"If that's how you want to play it." Drew opened the door but halted before Knox could make his escape to his room. "Cinderella story? Stella?"

"Yep, horrible past gives girl strength to hold on to an impossible and deteriorating dream. Now I just have to figure out how she gets her happily ever after for the story segment. You and Lori are the ones who told me this HEA, small-town stuff makes me more relatable." If he was being honest with himself, he wanted to give one woman a happily ever after the way he hadn't given Alima.

"Yeah, but remember this isn't really your segment. The producer said he had an angle, and that's what we're going to run with if you want him to pick up your show. Television streaming deal, remember?" Drew got out of the way, but his words were a serious obstacle to Knox's goals.

"Sure, whatever it takes, right?"

"Except you and I both know that no matter how much you try to act like a carefree person, you like to be in control of everything. What're you going to do if this sponsor says something you don't like?"

"It's business. I'll be fine," Knox told himself as much as Drew. It was part of the business, the ultimate goal to land a streaming deal and move out of Internet, but at what cost? He'd have zero say on his own show. The one he'd had total control in building and nurturing these past years.

"Lori's waiting. We need to get our team on the same page." Drew plopped down in the parlor where they'd already set up the laptops.

"Before that, we need to talk about something more pressing," Lori said before Knox could even reach the stairs. The tone of her voice made him stop in his tracks.

He unbuckled his belt, loosened his tie, removed his jacket, tossed it over the back of his chair, and collapsed into the springy, flower-covered seat. "Shoot."

Lori shuffled a few folders around, which told him she was stalling to get her courage up. Not good at all. "You might want to rethink the Cinderella angle you were talking about when you came in. It might be too, um…innocent."

A twitch of unease made him cross his leg, resting his ankle on his other knee. "Don't understand." He leaned forward, eyeing the folder she held in her hand. "Oh, you're talking about her father's arrest. No worries. We can still spin that." He collapsed back against the chair and stretched. "She already told me all about her mother and father and their less-than-stellar pasts. It'll only make the story spin better."

"You seem to know a lot about Stella for one dinner date."

He shrugged.

"Not denying it?" Drew asked.

"That I learned some things about her tonight? No. It's why I went, right?"

"No, that it was a date." Lori shrank back with folder placed in her lap. "There's something different about you."

He ran a hand through his over-gelled hair, his fingers catching in a few places. That shower was gonna feel amazing, if he ever escaped this room. "This is it, right? Drew's chance to abandon me for a better job, you and I rising to the next level of all this. Listen, I know you both have worked hard to make this all work. I might have been difficult at times—"

"At times?" Lori crossed her arms over her chest.

"Only because I wanted us all to have a good life that we controlled. None of us wanted to go work for corporate America, right?"

"Yet, that's what you're about to do." Drew said flatly.

"No, it's not."

Lori quirked her head to one side. "It kind of is. This deal you want to move into streaming, what do you think will happen when you turn your show over?"

"We'll have an easier life and better income. We won't have to beg for followers or always be out promoting this show. You can both slow down a little." Knox uncrossed his legs and wiped the wrinkles down his pants.

"You slow down? Not possible." Drew retrieved the folder from Lori and tossed it onto the table. "Then you'd have to face whatever you're running from."

Knox snatched the folder. "What's this?"

"Your Cinderella story." Lori sighed. "I'm sorry... I didn't want to find this, but you told me to dig deep. It's my job."

Knox flipped open the folder to a blown-up photo of a

young Stella, maybe fourteen, in a mug shot. His mouth went sandpit dry. "What for?"

"We don't know. Her juvie record's sealed. All we know is that she's been arrested. It could be nothing, but you told me to do a deep dive, so I did." She studied his face the way she did when he didn't communicate what he wanted and expected her to guess. "I'm sorry now that I did."

"Your job?" He cleared his throat. Why did Stella not tell him? He'd asked, and he'd thought she was strong enough to be honest. "Why?"

"Because, Knox, you want to work with this woman, despite how much you've protested about it. Despite how much she's different than any woman you've been around since I've met you. Despite the fact that you're actually still sitting here considering this Cinderella spin, even with the evidence in your hand."

He closed the file and tossed it back onto the table. "You're both the ones who said that the producer wants this, so that means I don't have a choice. A producer whose name I don't even know."

"Bradley," Lori said.

"If the Cinderella spin doesn't work, I'll find another angle. It's what I do. I'll impress this Bradley person like I wow my fans on a regular basis."

He'd heard enough of this disaster they'd brought him into. "You're the ones who insisted this town had all the answers. Well, all I'm seeing is a ton of questions." He snagged his jacket and stood.

"Don't worry, Knox. I'll figure this out. I'll go talk to Stella tomorrow," Lori offered in her sweet, I-got-your-back tone.

"Or I can ask Carissa," Drew offered, but as much as Knox didn't love losing his friend to a woman, he knew that would put a rift between a new budding relationship. One that made his best buddy happy.

"No, my show. I'll ask." He retrieved the folder. "This stays between us for now. Got it?"

"Got it," they answered in unison.

"Anything else?" Not that Knox wanted any more bad news in one evening.

"Just one more question." Drew stood and rounded the table to face Knox. "Do you want our silence to protect the show or to protect Stella?"

ELEVEN

The cold garage floor sent a chill through Stella's feet. Thank goodness it was getting warmer out and she wouldn't have to pay for heating the loft. She could survive no air conditioning, sleeping in the hammock down in the garage bay with the door open most nights in the summer. Someday, maybe she wouldn't have to rob the electric company to pay the water bill.

She shuffled to the coffeemaker and recoiled at the smell of day-old coffee. There wasn't time to make it into town for a caffeine run, so she'd have to make do since she was out of coffee grounds. At least she had a full belly from last night's dinner. She'd slept better than she had in a month.

"Hey, open up! I've got a special delivery from Mary-Beth," Felicia's voice called through the side window. The coffee whisperer must've known Stella needed a fix.

She unlocked and opened the door and then snagged the proffered cardboard cup, ripped out the stopper, and guzzled a few gulps.

"Glad you're happy to see me." Felicia came in and set her purse and jacket on the counter.

"Sorry. I'm just desperate to wake up quick before this

meeting today." Stella set her cup down, pulled her hair away from her face with a band, and then resumed drinking at a slower, more enjoyable rate. "Mmm, cinnamon and cocoa powder. Perfect. How does she do it?"

"Wish I knew." Felicia cradled her cup between her hands and inhaled. "Fresh mint for me today. A shot of calming wake-me-up."

"What are you doing here?" Stella hopped up on the counter and crossed her ankles, pointing at the lawn chair to invite Felicia to stay for a minute.

They'd been close once, but even after the regrouping of their old girl gang, the tension had remained.

"We chewed Jackie out. What she did was wrong to both you and Knox."

"Everyone?" Stella eyed the mediator of the bunch.

"I'm the one who busted her." Felicia raised her cup and took a sip. "You know she did it out of jealousy. Everything the girl does is out of jealousy."

Stella tapped her lid. "What does she have to be jealous about? She was raised on the right side of town, had parents who doted on her, a career in New York City, and money. Even now, with a failing business, she still manages to buy whatever she wants. I don't know how she does it. It's like she has a Mary Poppins bag of money."

"Divorce," Felicia said, as if talking about ordering new spark plugs.

Stella choked, spitting her coffee into droplets next to the oil stain. She wiped her mouth with the back of her sleeve and looked at Felicia. "Say what?"

Felicia settled on the counter next to Stella. "There are a few things you don't know about Jackie that she swore me to secrecy when she returned. The only reason I'm telling you this now is because I don't want you to hate her again. Our friendships and our town can't handle another rift in the Fabulous Five." She leaned over and shoulder-bumped Stella. "Besides, I don't want you to kill her at the dress shop later."

"Her store? Why would I go there?" Stella abandoned her seat, downed the last of her coffee, and then slammed the cup on the counter at Felicia's side as if she'd shot whiskey instead of a latte. "Not happening. I've got a busy day trying to schmooze some uppity-up while dealing with this show and saving my garage. There's nothing you can say that'll get me into her store now or any other day."

Felicia slid her purse strap over her arm and headed for the door. "It's for Ms. Horton's wedding. Remember her? The lady who is a second mother to us all?"

"That's today? The wedding isn't until fall." Stella grimaced and tossed her empty cup into the trash, wishing she had another drink.

"It's today." Felicia pointed to the oversize wall calendar the girls had put up over her sink to make sure she didn't forget any important dates after she was a no-show for their last two girls' night outs.

Stella glanced at the red script in Mary-Beth's swirly handwriting. "Fine. I'll be there. Can I call her Divorcee?"

"No, but she knows that I told you. After she heard that her plan backfired, she surrendered to the truth."

Stella headed for the loft to change for the big meeting in an hour. "What truth?"

Felicia slid her purse strap over her shoulder and headed for the door. "You're not ready to hear the truth. Don't worry. I'll keep Jackie out of the way for you."

"Don't even start with me. I've already got too much stress in my life. Keep her out of the way of what? What is that woman up to now?"

"Nothing. That's the point, and she won't be interfering. I

mean, after I heard at the coffee shop this morning from Lori how great the date with Knox went last night, I sent Carissa to make Jackie stand down."

Stella gripped the banister. Knox had told Lori they'd had a good date? Did that mean there would be another one—a real date this time? The coffee threatened to rise up in protest for being guzzled instead of savored. "Business dinner."

Felicia held the door open but didn't leave. "Call it what you want, but someone likes you."

The thought of a man like Knox Brevard liking her was the most ludicrous thing she'd ever heard...and pathetic. She wouldn't be the poor little girl the rich guy saved. "We have nothing in common. Don't be ridiculous."

"Opposites attract."

"We shared a burrito."

"Hey, love has to start somewhere." Felicia waved over her shoulder but retreated at Talladega speed.

Stella didn't have time to contemplate the musings of Felicia and the girls, so she showered and changed while she thought about the gentleman who'd hung out in her garage and opened up to her last night. A man nothing like who she'd expected. Maybe he would come through on this show and she could save her *abuelo's* garage after all.

A pounding on the front door startled her, causing her heart to race. "Who's there?" she called out, running down the stairs and eyeing the wall clock. She still had twenty minutes before Knox and the sponsor would arrive.

No one answered. The person only pounded again. She hesitated. The only person who had ever beat on the door like that had been her father—a man she never wanted to see again— but he was in jail for a long time.

"Open up. We need to talk." Knox's voice penetrated the metal barrier.

Stella unlocked the door and found Knox dressed in a perfect suit, with perfectly gelled hair, but he wasn't wearing his perfected smile.

"What's wrong? What's going on?" Stella asked, stepping out of the way as Knox marched through the doorway, into the center of the garage, halted, and faced her.

"You said I could trust you."

Stella shut the door, feeling like she'd been called to Ms. Horton's office in ninth grade for setting the trash can on fire. "I don't know what this is about, but I'm an honest person. Abrupt but honest."

"Then why'd you lie to me?" His gaze looked more hurt than angry, the way his eyes softened, but his voice sounded harsh.

Her hackles raised at his tone. "I don't lie, and I have no idea what you're talking about. Is this a new game you're playing?"

"This is no game. This is my career." Knox cornered her between the lever to the lift and the toolbox. "You knew what happened with the last story I did with a garage... This was supposed to make up for that, but now... Now I need you to be straight with me so I might be able to get ahead of this. Manage the fallout."

Stella fisted her hands and brushed passed him. "Listen here. You're not welcome in my garage anymore. You want to spout things at me, then explain and ask a question. I'm not one of your bimbo minions you can order around."

"Fine." Knox didn't back down like most men. Instead, he marched up to her and pulled something out of his pocket, unfolded it, and held it out to her. "Explain this."

Stella saw it. The one secret she'd managed to bury even from the residents of Sugar Maple, even from her friends. She swallowed the fear and agony of the past, lifted her chin, and said, "I can't."

TWELVE

The garage air was thick with engine oil, old fumes, and lies. "How could you keep this from me?" Knox flashed the mug shot at her again and then tossed it on the hood of the old Chevy. "I thought you were different than the other women who would lie to get on the Knox Brevard show. I guess I was wrong."

"I don't lie." Stella turned her back to him, but not fast enough. He saw it, the regret in her eyes. "I didn't want to do your show, remember?"

"I asked you if you had anything in your past that could damage my show. You said no."

She spun on him, her arms stiff by her side. "There's nothing."

"Are you trying to tell me this isn't real? That you didn't have a mug shot taken when you were...what? Fourteen?"

"Thirteen." Stella's voice dipped, as did her chin. "I did have a mug shot, but it didn't happen."

"What are you talking about?" Knox fought the anxiety and disappointment. This shouldn't be hitting him so hard. This girl lied and deceived him. She didn't deserve his understanding and compassion.

She shot to the hood of the car and snatched the picture. Her face was red, and the lines of an elder with regrets appeared around her eyes. "Where did you get this?"

"The thing in your hand that doesn't exist?" Knox huffed. "From Lori. I told her to look for anything in your past that could cause harm to my show."

"You didn't trust me?" Stella asked, as if she had a right to be upset that he'd discovered her truth.

"Good thing I didn't. I can't believe I thought this would work. That you were different. Honest." His arms, back, and attitude stiffened.

"I am." Stella continued to study the picture in her hands. "How did she find this? It doesn't exist."

"Stop saying that and start explaining since you're holding proof in your hand that it does exist and that you were arrested." She had to be lying and hiding some teenage indiscretion. If he was right, what else was she hiding?

"I wasn't." Stella walked to the sink, dropped the photo into it, lit a match, and burned the picture. Smoke drifted into the air, along with the chemical odor from the photo paper.

"Burning it won't make it disappear." Knox eyed the clock, his watch, and then the clock again. "You need to tell me everything now while you still can. Bradley, the television producer, will be here any minute. If I don't know what this is all about, then I will pull the plug on all of this."

Stella looked smaller, less like an Amazon warrior and more like a sad princess stuck in a tower. "So, you're saying if I don't tell you about something that didn't happen, then our deal for the show is over?"

He straightened his tie and adjusted his jacket. "Yes."

"Then it's over." The princess morphed into an evil queen, the way Stella's eyes blazed and her jaw set with determination.

A car pulled up outside. "Wait, no. You can't do this. The

producer's here. Just tell me what this is all about so I'll know how to deal with it. I'll fix it. I promise."

"No." Stella blinked away what looked like tears. "You're not my hero, and you can't fix everything."

Knox wanted to know what happened, but she wasn't budging. The car door slammed outside. "Tell me this. Did you commit a crime that will damage our show? Did you cheat, commit fraud, get arrested for drugs?"

"No."

He paced the floor, eyeing the tall man headed for the door. The train for his future had arrived, and he didn't want to miss the ride. "Grand larceny, arson?"

"No and no." Stella looked him straight in the eye without blinking. She was telling the truth, but was it because he hadn't asked the right question?

If he pulled the plug now and then discovered later that he'd made a mistake, he'd regret it for a long time. This was too big, and he needed more intel before making any major decisions. For now, he'd chalk it up to an adolescent indiscretion that was a lesson learned.

"We'll move forward with Bradley for now, but you and I need to talk more later." Knox went to the door to greet the man who promised him a better future.

"Not about this, we won't. Trust me or don't, it's your choice, but all I ask is that you keep your Hollywood trap shut. It never happened, so no one in town needs to know. Got it?"

"No promises."

The man's footsteps creaked the porch steps.

"Then I walk here and now." Stella crossed her arms over her chest, and he saw her determination. Whatever had happened, it was so bad she would rather do anything than admit the truth.

"Stay at least until this meeting's over, and then we'll talk more. I promise not to say anything to anyone about your record until after we speak." The knock at the door made his breath catch. "Let's just hear him out, and then we'll talk."

She nodded, but he could see her hesitation. He'd planned to come here and ask her about her past, ease into what had happened when she was younger, but instead, he'd resorted to his old commanding ways.

For a second, he wanted to pull her into a hug and soothe whatever brought tears to her eyes. A woman like Stella didn't cry easily, not in front of anyone. Not that she'd shed a tear, but he'd seen them.

Stella turned on the faucet, and the smoke disappeared, although the caustic odor of burned film remained behind.

Knox straightened his tie and opened the door. "Hello. Welcome."

"I wasn't sure I was in the right place for a moment." The man offered his hand. "I'm Bradley Houlster."

"Nice to meet you. I'm Knox Brevard, and over there is Stella Frayser."

The man didn't take his hand. Instead, he darted through the entryway, straight to Stella. "Hello. It's a pleasure to meet such a beautiful woman." The man bent over and kissed her knuckles. Great, he was a rich Casanova. Stella would probably slug him two minutes into their meeting.

"Nice to meet you." Stella slipped her hand away and looked to Knox.

He raced to her aid. "I know you wanted to meet here so you could see the place, but why don't we take a quick look around and then head to the coffee shop to sit and chat."

Bradley spun around, eyeing all the different corners of the garage. "Is that a 1957 Chevy?"

Stella lit up like a flare in the night sky. "Yes."

"Original?" Bradley ran his hand down the side of the car.

"Yes. Down to the original switches, steering, and emblem pieces." Stella reached through the open window and pointed to the dashboard. "Even the original radio. No way I'm going to put something else into this car."

"You're a restoration purist?"

"All the way."

What was happening? Knox clapped his hands together. "Now that you've seen the garage, let's—"

"You know, I have a 1972 Porsche 916."

Stella smacked him on the arm. "No way. They only made like twelve of those."

"You know your classics." Bradley shot an endearing playboy smile at her. Did she notice they were all caps?

"It's all I care about."

"Then why do you want to do a Knox Brevard show?" Bradley leaned into Stella, making sure his elbow touched her. A rookie move, but when he reached around her to dust off something behind her, Knox saw the man was a player of the worst kind.

Knox cleared his throat. "It'll help save her business."

"A business she doesn't really enjoy as much as car restoration from what I can tell. Why don't I take you for that coffee and we'll discuss classic cars?" Bradley flipped his thousand-dollar-cut hair.

Stella looked to Knox. "I, um…" She straightened and took a step away from Bradley. "The show is about the garage. It was my grandfather's, and I love it here. Classic cars are my hobby, but this garage is my business."

Knox forced his instant dislike for the man under control before he lost his temper and it cost him the streaming deal. "Perhaps we can all go for coffee and talk about the show."

Bradley opened the driver's door, popped the hood, opened it, and leaned over the engine. "No need. I've already had my team research your show. I have everything I need about you and the platform for the series I'm proposing. It isn't overly complicated. What I don't know yet is everything about this garage and this intriguing woman who runs it. I like to know what I'm investing in since I only produce winning shows. You should go get that coffee. We can talk later, Bronx. Have Lori put something on my calendar."

"It's Knox. And Lori set this time for us to discuss the show."

"No. There's been some sort of misunderstanding. I didn't come all this way to talk to you. I came to talk to Stella. She's the reason I'm here."

THIRTEEN

The coffeehouse was unusually quiet, but it was early afternoon. Stella cupped her mug and inhaled the eye-opening brew Mary-Beth had concocted as if she'd known Stella hadn't slept all night.

"Tell us how this morning went. I heard there was drama." Jackie crossed her legs, her heels so tall they looked like stilts extending out of her feet. The woman had to suffer greatly to be in fashion all the time. No thanks. Combat boots were durable and comfortable.

"No drama here. I don't look for attention-seeking issues the way some people do." Stella fought her lip curling with anger and shot Felicia a warning stare. How could she have added coffee social for the friend group on top of dress fitting? Too much to ask for one morning.

"Oh, hon." Mary-Beth nudged the mug full of steaming liquid with white froth on top toward Stella. "When are you going to believe we only want to help? Tell us what happened."

Carissa tucked her feet together under the bistro chair, crossing her ankles. "Drew said Knox arrived at the office in a state worse than he'd ever seen him. Something about some egocentric man swooping into town and dismissing Knox."

"I told you he liked you." Felicia smiled so bright, Stella wanted to put duct tape over it.

"Don't be stupid." She wrapped her fingers around the coffee cup. Mary-Beth had served her coffee in the ceramic mug that the Fabulous Five had made in high school. Anytime someone had a bad day, they'd all meet, and the person who was suffering was presented the cup of love with its nauseating hearts and smiles. And Stella's gray cloud that Felicia had put pink dots on to make it happier. How many times had Stella drunk coffee from this cup during her troubled times in high school? Maybe if she'd trusted the girls when she was thirteen, she wouldn't have been in the situation that ended in a mug shot. "Knox didn't like the fact that Bradley is into cars and cared more about my Chevy than discussing Knox's new show."

"Ouch." Mary-Beth tapped her turquoise-painted nail against her mug. "He wouldn't take that well."

Felicia scooted her chair closer without touching Stella. "Listen, we all want this show to happen, but we also know you will hate doing it. Is it worth it?"

"I'll be fine. I can handle Knox Brevard and his hot air balloon–sized head." Stella eyed each of them, tempted to dredge up the past and confess her worst nightmares, but she couldn't do it. The looks of pity followed by the reprimands for not sharing, followed by sleepovers and hair braiding would be too much. No way, no how. It had been easier to focus on each of the other girls' issues over the years. She almost wished that Jackie would steal another fiancé so they could go back to strained conversations and distance. Things were always easier when you didn't get too close to people. Although, since the one closest to engagement was Carissa, that would be beyond friendship breaking. It would be life-ending.

"What are you keeping from us, Stella Frayser?" Jackie crossed her arms over her chest and angled her chin with that diva way she did.

"Nothing." Stella lifted the mug to her nose and inhaled nutmeg and something else that was equally as soothing, but she couldn't identify its aroma. "I told you, Knox didn't like being dismissed for a car."

"The injustice of it!" Jackie pressed her hand to her forehead in a mock faint. "We should all be so lucky to have men fighting over us."

"Not what happened, and unlike you, I don't need men fighting over me to prove I'm worth something." Stella almost felt bad for her harsh words, but Jackie always nudged until Stella blew. She deserved it, though, after she set Stella's meeting with Knox up for failure with a doll dress and cow slab. Besides, hostility was their communication of choice.

"How did Knox handle that?" Felicia asked, leaning forward in her chair with her elbows on her knees and cup at chin level, as if to shield Jackie from Stella's anger.

"I don't know. He was quiet after that. It was uncomfortable. I don't do uncomfortable."

"You don't do anything that requires human emotion." Jackie shifted her chair to make eye contact around Felicia's friend block.

Stella ignored her and focused on the others. "Bradley kept me focused on the car, and then he told me about owning a 1972 Porsche 916. Knox was quiet."

Carissa chuckled. "I take it that's cool?"

"Cool? They only made 12 of them ever." Stella abandoned her mug on the table. "Seriously, do you guys ever listen to me when I talk shop?"

"No," Jackie said with a dismissive wave. "I'd say Knox took it bad, then."

"Why would you say that?" Mary-Beth asked.

"Because Knox is never quiet. In all the time we've spent together, he's always been boisterous and animated and loves attention in public." Jackie's smile said she related to Knox's behavior.

Stella knew the two of them were much better suited for each other. Knox was never and would never be her man. She'd been distracted by his moments of humanity, but the man still only cared about his show and the fame that came with it. She didn't have time for that, not when she needed to save her shop. "If you want Knox, you can have him. Not interested."

Jackie snickered. "He's not even on my radar, dear."

"What did Bradley say about why he came here to speak with you?" Felicia asked.

"He didn't." Stella let out a big breath she'd been holding since Knox had arrived in town with his idea of doing a story on her shop. "Bradley's phone rang, and he darted out before he finished sharing information with Knox or me."

"Why aren't you both asking her the important question?" Jackie rested her elbows on the table and her fists under her chin and batted her eyelashes.

"What question's that?" Felicia asked before Stella could kick her under the table so she wouldn't get snagged on Jacqueline's baited hook.

"Is the rich car guy handsome?" Jackie asked, continuing to bat her eyelashes.

Stella smacked her face with her palms and groaned. She ran her hands down to her chin and then dropped them onto her lap. "Who cares? I don't want to deal with another uppity, self-absorbed person in my life. I don't want to do Knox's show. All I want is a little extra work for my garage. Is that too much to ask?"

Jackie obviously got the meaning behind her words. "Better than being a greasy hermit."

Felicia shot up out of her chair. "We best get going to your shop for our dress fittings. Ms. Horton should be off work now."

The moderator of their group apparently worked her magic, because Jackie glanced at her designer watch with a diamond bezel and shot up. "You're going to love your dresses. Banana yellow with fuchsia belt and puffed sleeves." She darted out of the coffee shop before any of them could react.

"Please tell me she's joking," Carissa mumbled.

"If not, this greasy hermit might break in and cut those dresses up for shop rags."

"For once, I'll join your felonious plan." Felicia took a long drink and then put her cup down.

"We should get a move on. We don't want to keep Ms. Horton waiting. After all, she's been waiting a lifetime to marry Mr. Strickland." Carissa stood, pushing her chair in and wiping down the table. "Hey, Stella. I'll ask Lori if she's heard anything."

"I bet if there's something to find, she'll know how to uncover it," Stella said with a bitterness that could sour sugar.

"Whoo. Got a problem with Lori now, too?" Jackie asked.

"No. No problem at all." Stella couldn't explain the issue without it leading to more explanations of things she didn't want anyone finding out about her. She'd spent the last fifteen or so years hiding that memory from everyone, including herself. She wouldn't even think about it, let alone say it aloud. How could she explain to her friends and everyone else that she'd been arrested at thirteen for solicitation?

FOURTEEN

Knox stood at the office window overlooking the town square. He spotted Felicia, Carissa, Mary-Beth, and Stella headed from the coffee shop to Jackie's dress store. According to Lori, they were being fitted for dresses for the mayor's wedding. It wasn't until fall, so he didn't understand the rush.

"I spoke with Bradley." Lori's voice carried from the small kitchen off the office, but it wasn't enough to draw his gaze from the beautiful spring day outside into the damp and dreary room.

"Yeah."

"He said that he didn't expect Stella to be so engaging and he wants to get to know her better." Lori giggled. "He's a smooth talker, isn't he?"

"Yeah, as smooth as a jagged rock landslide," he mumbled, catching one last glimpse of Stella before she rounded the corner at the end of the street and disappeared out of view. "He's talking about giving her a big-money job restoring an old car. That gives her a way out of my show."

"You really think that will change her mind?" Lori asked.

"Yeah." He moved from the window and plopped down at the desk. "Tell me again what Bradley said."

"He said he's sticking around to observe this show and will make a final decision about your production with his network."

"Great," he said. His voice trailed off along with his thoughts of a better future.

Lori huffed. "Listen, he's a car guy and thinks Stella is charismatic enough to win over an audience. If you can't convince her to do the show, maybe Bradley can."

"I'll convince Stella." Knox picked up a pencil and rolled it between his fingers.

Lori narrowed her gaze. "If you think you can."

"The woman is unpredictable, bossy, and a...a...vegetarian. But she's still a woman, which is my specialty."

"I don't think we have to tell your viewers she's a vegetarian. You're safe on that one." Lori chuckled. "I guess I need to ask the real question here."

"What's that?"

"Did she sign the paperwork to do the show?" Lori asked. "And you trust her that whatever the mugshot was about is safe and won't blow up in our faces later?"

The pencil snapped between his fingers, and he dropped them onto the desk. "I can't help her if she's not honest with me. We have plausible deniability. If it comes out, she's on her own and we wash our hands of her."

Lori's face softened, and she lowered to the chair on the other side of the desk. "You wouldn't." She took the broken yellow wood pieces and tossed them into the trash. "You would never do that." She held his hands and squeezed them. In all the years they'd worked together, she'd never done that. "It's time to stop pushing everyone away to protect yourself."

He analyzed her gaze that erupted in pity and other equally uncomfortable emotions. "You know about Alima." The words stung his throat, his lungs, his soul.

"Yes."

He jerked his hands away and bolted from his chair, pacing and cursing under his breath. "How?"

"I find out things, remember?" Lori winked as if she were talking about some tea party, not the loss of the woman he loved.

"Drew?" He entwined his fingers behind his head and leaned back, trying to get air as if he'd finished a sprint.

"He doesn't know that I know of. It's not my place to tell him. I would never share your secret." She remained in her chair, giving him space. Smart lady.

"How long?"

"What?"

He turned and dropped his arms to his side. "How long have you known?"

"Since the downward turn on your reputation started tanking the ratings of your show." Lori studied her fingers in her lap. "It's my job to keep you on top. I dug into your past to find a way to spin things in your favor."

"But you didn't use it?" He took in a cleansing, newfound-trust kind of breath. "Despite the ratings and the possible loss of all of our careers, you didn't even ask to use it."

"No." Lori shook her head and looked up at him, tears in her eyes. "Some things aren't meant for the world to know. That kind of pain is private, but it doesn't have to be carried alone." She stood and took a step toward him, but he cringed away.

The one time he couldn't let any person close to him was when he was speaking of, thinking of, or remembering Alima.

"I'm here if you ever want to talk. If not, you should talk to someone."

"It's the past. No need to talk about it now. There's no way to change it or fix it, so no reason to rehash it."

Lori looked to her watch. "I need to head over to the dress store. Mayor Horton asked me to join the girls. Apparently, she has been trying to make me part of the girls' team in town for a while and I've resisted. Now, though, I think I want to entertain the idea of hanging around this town in the future. There's something special about this place. I know it, Drew knows it, and even you know it. Even if you won't admit it to yourself."

He waved her away, ready for the conversation to end.

"You know, it's okay to keep the past away unless it is destroying your future."

"What's that supposed to mean?"

Lori headed to the door in a quick retreat. "You know you think you don't deserve Stella, and maybe you don't."

"Thanks. That makes me feel so much better. Glad we had this chat." Knox returned to the front window, begrudgingly drawn to the goings-on of this little town.

"Ask yourself one thing though. Have you ever been cruel to a woman? Yes, you've played games with women who wanted to play and knew the rules. You'd never drag someone unknowingly into drama."

Lori approached, and Knox pressed his palm to the windowsill to brace himself for what she was leading into with this conversation.

"So?"

"So, Stella is innocent. The strong, abrasive exterior of a girl like that... Some might think she can handle the manipulation, but perhaps she's hiding as much pain as you are. What if whatever that mugshot is about will dredge up great pain for her? She isn't aware of the risk she's taking. I know you, Knox. You would never intentionally cause anyone pain to get what you want."

"You think too highly of me," Knox grumbled.

"Maybe, but Stella sees something in you that has gotten her attention. I'd say she's a good judge of character. I hate to see your hesitation to let her closer cost you a fantastic opportunity."

"I can't stop her working on his car for money instead of my show."

"You can. Just open your heart." With those final words, Lori retreated. Her steps echoed from the stairs, telling Knox he'd finally be alone. He gripped the window's molding and rested his head on the cool glass. He watched her cross the town square and head to Jackie's store.

Despite his desire to win this deal, he knew Stella was innocent in all of this. Perhaps if he told her the score. That if whatever didn't happen becomes public, it could change her life forever. If he did that, he'd lose her from the show, and it would cost him the deal with Bradley. Could he risk so much for a woman who didn't even trust him with her truth? Lori was wrong. Stella wasn't blinded by any misguided feelings for him. She was tough and able to handle anything. And there was no need to muck things up with unwanted feelings for some girl in a small town. He'd been there, done that. It might have been thousands of miles away. The scenery was different, the customs different, the rules of engagement different, but the scenario was hauntingly similar.

He was not at all eager to go back.

FIFTEEN

The girls chatted like they were old friends who had never been torn apart by lies and deceit. Was it all for Ms. Horton's benefit, or could they be a Fabulous Five again? Stella found herself sipping champagne, the bubbles tickling her nose. For the briefest of times, she thought that she could enjoy a finer life full of rich things.

Felicia and Mary-Beth were fluttering around Ms. Horton's dress and pointing out all the amazing details Jackie had incorporated into the design. Even though the shiny beading wasn't Stella's taste, she had to give Jackie a thumbs-up on her creation. "It's perfect," Stella mumbled under her breath.

They all stopped midsip, midturn, midsentence.

"What?" Stella abandoned her crystal glass on the side table.

"You said something's perfect?" Carissa's eyes were wide and her smile even bigger.

"About one of my designs," Jackie said with a straight pin hanging from the side of her lips.

"So?" Stella shifted in the plush seat.

Felicia collapsed on the chair at her side. "You never say

anything's perfect. It might be fine, average, okay, acceptable, but never perfect."

Mary-Beth grabbed the champagne flute. "What did you put in her drink, Jackie?"

"Stop. You're all being ridiculous." Stella grabbed her jacket and flung it over her shoulder. "I've gotta get back to the shop."

Ms. Horton hiked her dress up and hobbled over to block Stella's escape. "Nope. Not happening. Sit back down. This is my fitting, and you're going to stay put."

Stella backed away, seeing a hint of the legend of bridezilla making an appearance. "Okay, I'll stay. It's fine."

"Now that's the Stella we know and love." Carissa winked. "I think you should let out the hips a little, though. Mr. Strickland said that he wanted to dance like Fred Astaire and Ginger Rogers at their wedding. Ms. Horton can't even take a step left or right without pulling the hem to her knees."

"Point taken." Jackie waved Ms. Horton back to the wedding gown platform.

Stella wanted to thank Carissa for throwing the distraction in to get everyone off her case. The front door opened, sending a whiff of honeysuckle inside from the plants beginning to bloom out front of the shop. Stella always found it to be a pleasant aroma from a distance, but the flower was too potent if within fifty feet.

"Hi, ladies. I hope it's okay. Mayor Horton invited me." Lori entered with a soft step and voice. Stella couldn't help but resent the woman after discovering she was the one who had uncovered her adolescent mug shot. That had been squashed and buried along with the memory that only she and Ms. Horton knew about. Not even Carissa had ever discovered the ugly truth, despite Ms. Horton's push toward Stella telling the girls while they were in high school. Eventually, she gave up and let it go and they'd all moved on. No reason to dredge up the dirty secrets of the past...until now.

"Come on in." Ms. Horton opened her arms and welcomed Lori as one of Sugar Maple's own. Stella cringed at the thought. The sooner Lori left, the sooner Stella could stop worrying about everyone finding out.

They all fussed and fawned over Ms. Horton, the dress, the wedding, and the epic tale of ex-high school sweetheart turned middle-aged groom.

Stella had never understood why people thought the story was romantic. The man married another woman, despite the fact that he was doing the right thing by helping a friend from being run out of town for an unwanted pregnancy in a time that apparently you had to wear a scarlet letter for the sin. Did it really matter why? The man had broken Ms. Horton's heart. He'd done the wrong thing, despite the right reasons.

"I think the dress is perfect," Lori squealed.

They all looked to Stella.

"That seems to be the word of the day," Ms. Horton said with a smile.

Carissa turned Ms. Horton to face the three-way mirror. "Look at yourself. You are perfect. Mr. Strickland is going to forget how to dance or even speak when he sees you in this dress."

"Might not be too long until we see you in a dress like that, Carissa." Lori twirled her finger in the air like a magic wand. "I'm just saying... I've never seen Drew so enamored by anyone before. He's head over heels for you, girl."

Carissa blushed.

How sweet.

Stella tried to be happy for her friend—and she'd made progress—but everything was changing, and if there was one thing Stella didn't like, it was change.

Lori settled in next to Stella and set her purse on the floor at her feet. "Hi, you. I've been wanting to talk to you."

"Sounds like you've been talking a lot lately," Stella said, leaving a bitterness on her tongue long after the words were said.

"I wanted to speak to you, but Knox insisted he deal with it. Listen, I'm really sorry. I didn't mean to cause any trouble for you. Knox told me to dig, so I did."

"All the way to hell apparently," Stella grunted. Her leg bounced fast and hard, energy raced through her, and she wanted to run from the room.

"I'm sorry. If it makes you feel any better, I stopped digging. All he knows is that you have a mug shot."

Stella grabbed her hand and squeezed tight. "Not here."

Lori looked between her and the girls.

"Everything all right over there, ladies?" Jackie asked, her gaze on Stella's hands.

"Ouch." Ms. Horton jumped. "You stuck me. Pay attention to yourself when you're jabbing those things into the dress.

Stella retracted her hand, and Lori rubbed her wrist. "Understood." The woman looked like she wanted to run as badly as Stella did.

"All finished. You can take the dress off." Jackie removed the pincushion from her wrist. The minute Ms. Horton entered the dressing room, Stella snagged her jacket.

"Okay, girl time's over. I've got to go. Business meeting," Stella said.

"You're lying so you can get out of here," Jackie accused.

Stella huffed. "Weren't you listening earlier, I have to meet up with Bradley about his classic car."

Lori snagged her purse. "No, actually, she does. We need to get contracts signed for the next show, so she needs to meet with Bradley about more than just the car."

"Wow, our little Stella a movie star." Jackie tossed the pincushion into a basket.

Stella hoofed it toward the door before anyone could see the utter shock on her face. "You heard the lady." It was obvious Lori had tried to throw her an olive branch but smacked her in the face instead.

"Don't forget we're meeting Sunday evening for another girls' night at my house," Mary-Beth hollered.

"Right. Sure." Stella raced out the door and across the town square with her head down, hoping to make it back to her shop without any more surprises.

"Are you going to sell yourself?" Knox's voice shot through her like an armor-piercing bullet.

She stopped, realizing he sat on the bench in the center of the square. His words sucker-punched her. "How did you figure it out?" Stella choked on her words and the shame. "Lori said she didn't dig any deeper. How?" Her voice cracked. For the first time since she was thirteen, she wanted to cry. To shout at the world for the deck she'd been handed.

She pushed up her sleeves and marched toward him.

He shot his hands up. "Wait."

"No, you wait. Who gave you the right to dig into my past? What makes you people think you can come in here and destroy people's lives? That's what you've done. You've dug up the most painful thing in my life and thrown it in my face. If you don't want to do the show with me because my father tried to sell me to a man for drugs, then that's your business. I was a child. I didn't know. I didn't! I didn't..."

He put his arms around her and pulled her toward him. She balled up her fists and tried to punch him, to punch the memory away, but he was too strong. "Let go of me." She managed to shove hard enough that she let her go. "I need to go stop Lori one way or another. This entire town doesn't need to know my dirty little secret. Even if I have to beat it out of her."

"Lori didn't tell me."

Stella froze. "I don't understand." She sucked in a short breath. "How did you figure it out?"

"I didn't." Knox approached, this time slower, tentatively. "You told me."

"What?" Stella fisted her hands again. She wanted to hit anything, anyone. No, her father. The man who'd betrayed her, manipulated her. "I didn't tell you. You're twisting things."

"No, I'm not." He lowered his voice. "I asked if you were going to sell yourself."

"Right. Like when I was thirteen."

Knox placed his fingers on her forearm. "No. I never would've said something like that if I had known."

"You said..."

"I know. And I shouldn't have said it, but all I meant was that I thought that you were selling yourself to him by restoring his car to save your garage without having to do my show. It was wrong to say, and I didn't mean it. I was angry. I only meant that you didn't have to pick that option. I'll work with you to save your garage."

"Why should I trust you?" Her insides felt like an engine with bad oil, telling her to run, to never trust anyone. The same thing she'd been doing since she was thirteen. Never allowing a man close to her except her *abuelo*. "Why should I trust any man to help me when I couldn't even trust my own father?"

SIXTEEN

"I'm so sorry." Knox rubbed his forehead, wishing to forget the pain in Stella's eyes. Anger bubbled up inside him, but he knew going off the rails wouldn't help her. "You said your father's in jail, right?"

"Yes." She looked toward the afternoon sky, as if to fly away. "I put him there."

"Good for you. That took more strength than most woman could muster. Heck, most men."

"Good for me?" Stella slapped her palms against her thighs with a muted smack to her jeans. "What kid does that? You should've heard him when they carried him away." Stella took off up the sidewalk toward her garage. A car came barreling down the hill, so Knox grabbed her elbow to keep her from stepping out in front of it. She turned on him. "He said I was a worthless, ungrateful little whore who didn't deserve him as a father, didn't deserve a father at all, and that he wasn't even my real father. Only a man my mother dropped me off with when she didn't want me anymore."

She spun on her heels again, her hair smacking him in the face, and marched up the hill. "He's the one who didn't deserve you." Knox ran to catch her. For a small woman, she sure was fast and feisty. They reached the gravel lot outside the garage, and he didn't want her to run off that upset, so he got in front of her, blocking her path. "Wait. Just stop for a second."

To his surprise, she halted. Her Latino attitude covered her expression—her face looked hot-chili red.

He took her right hand and held it between his, close to his heart. "What happened to you is unforgiveable. A father is meant to protect his little girl, not put her in harm's way. I'm glad your father's in jail, or I might consider ruining him my new mission in life."

"Why would you do that?"

He pressed her palm to his chest. "Do you feel that?"

Stella's eyebrows rose. "Your heart?"

"Yes. You feel how fast that's beating? That's because I want to go murder your father. I'm a soldier to the core. Protecting others was ingrained in me for many years."

Stella grinned. "You know you're strange, right? You don't even know me."

"I do know you, Stella."

She chuckled, but her breath quickened. "Please. We've spent a few hours together. You don't know me at all."

"I know that you like spicy food. You don't want to do this show, but you want to save your garage because your grandfather took you in when your parents left. You're a loyal friend to Carissa, and from what I understand, you still hold ill feelings toward Jacqueline for stealing Carissa's fiancé years ago. You are strong and brave and beautiful."

Stella slipped her fingers from his grasp. "See, you don't know me at all. I'm plain, combative, irritable, and I would prefer to be in work overalls than fancy heels."

He expected her to take off again, but she didn't. Instead,

she studied her dark boots, nudging little white rocks around. "Listen. You need to make me a promise."

"What's that?"

"You can't tell anyone about my father." Stella looked up at him, lifting her chin high and proud. "No one in town knows except Ms. Horton."

"Why?" Knox ran his finger along her hairline, tucking the few stray strands behind her ear and then trailed them down her rosy, soft cheek.

"Because, I don't need everyone knowing my business. Besides, they'd all be mad at me for not telling them all those years ago. I couldn't, though."

"Why?" he asked.

"You wouldn't understand."

"Let me try. You didn't want to tell anyone because you didn't want people to look at you differently? Because you didn't want pity or people trying to be overly kind to you because you had suffered? Because you wanted to forget while everyone else would want to talk about it?"

Stella's eyes went wide, and then she closed them and took a deep breath. "Listen. Just don't tell anyone."

"I won't."

Stella brushed past him. "I wish I could trust you, but you're a man."

"I am, but not all men are liars. I am who I am, but I don't lie about it."

She unlocked the door and walked inside, leaving it wide open for him to follow, so he took his cue. She grabbed two waters from the mini-fridge and tossed one at him.

"And who are you, Knox?"

"I'm someone who doesn't want to see you get hurt anymore."

"How can I trust you?" Stella said, biting her lip. "I mean, you have a record with women and shows. You care more about fame than anything else in life."

"I would never lie or manipulate to get a woman on my arm for that photo opportunity. Any woman you've ever seen on my arm used me as much as I used her. She wanted to climb the entertainment ladder by using my platform, and I'd use her to make my fans believe I was a—"

"Womanizing creep?"

"Harsh." He unscrewed the top on the water bottle. "Player is the word I was going for."

"Told you I was irritable and combative." Stella smiled before she took a sip of her own water. "You're worried I'm not going to do your show because of the car offer from Bradley."

"Are you?" Knox set his water on the counter and crossed his arms, feeling his anger bubbling again.

"I never wanted to be on television. I'm not right for the job. You're wrong for me, and I don't have time to wait to see if your show puts my garage on the Internet map." She looked frightened but guarded. "I was going to sell my *abuelo's* car so that I could get the money to buy a computer so that I could fix modern cars, something I never wanted to do, but if I got enough business in time, I could save this place."

"I see. We'll do the show about car restoration, and I'll pay you in advance for the show," Knox offered.

Stella laughed, a defensive kind of snort. "Your show doesn't work that way, remember? And even if we filmed about car restoration, it isn't the subject that keeps me from wanting to do the show, it is the price that fame claims on a person's life. Besides, I don't need the money. Bradley says he's bringing his 916 here so that I can restore it and he's paying me top dollar. Once I get her done, I'll have enough to catch up on the rent on this place."

"How much do you need?" Knox asked.

"Don't you dare reach for your wallet. I'm not looking for handouts, just work. I don't need a man playing hero to rescue me." Stella huffed and downed the rest of her water.

"Fine. We'll figure this out, but trust me. Bradley will take too long too, and I'm here now. I can deliver on my promise. Can Bradley?"

Honk. Honk.

"Expecting someone?"

Stella raced to the large garage door and pulled the chain. "Yes, it's Bradley in the 916, delivering on his promise."

SEVENTEEN

A few minutes later, after Knox had excused himself with mention of another important meeting he needed to attend, Bradley strutted around inside Stella's garage with a pinched face. Stella couldn't help but think the man looked like the Ken doll Jackie had when they were kids: stiff, faux tan, and plastic. He eyed the kitchen counter, brushed it with his hand as if her garage was so dirty he'd be tainted by touching something, and then leaned against it. "Tell me, how long have you owned this place?" His gaze traveled around the roof line, corners, and to the floor, all the time his lip curling in disapproval.

"My entire life, you could say. Well, since I moved in with my grandparents as a young girl." She found herself speaking as if she were Jackie at a fashion show in Paris.

"Grandparents raised you, huh?"

Stella stiffened at the thought of his questions leading to something she didn't want to share, something that Knox already knew. Would he tell anyone? Her stomach gurgled with nauseating acid. If he did, she'd never be able to face her friends and the town when they knew her shame.

"I was raised by boarding schools. Great education, allowed

me to meet all the right people," he said in a matter-of-fact tone, as if he'd been asked.

"Why don't we take a look at the engine to see what we're dealing with mechanically." Stella headed for the 916's hood release.

Bradley rounded the car, meeting her by the driver's-side door. "I did my research, and you have limited experience but your work is impeccable. I expect my cars to be restored to perfection."

"How do you know I'm accomplished? You've never seen me work."

He tilted his head at the Chevy. "That's quality restoration."

"You judged my ability on one car?"

"I have a confession to make. When I found out you were one of the options for Knox's show, I researched you and discovered your classic car business and had to check you out. Knox has you to thank, since you moved up the timetable of my offer to him. I'd planned on waiting to see how this season went for him before offering him the show with me."

"Researched me?" What was everyone's fascination with her, and how much had he dug up? Did Lori share what she'd found with the mug shot? "Not an interesting endeavor, I'm sure."

"It wasn't until I caught a glimpse of you during the segment filmed about the bakery. Then I researched former repairs and car restorations and ran across an old Thunderbird you did. It looked brand-new."

"That was two years ago." Stella recalled the project with fond memories. It wasn't often she had the opportunity to restore cars more than just fix them. "Two cars... Not really a good enough sample to statistically decide I'm a good mechanic."

"I don't know if you're a good mechanic. I said you're great at car restorations, and that's what I want your show to focus on." He walked around the car, studying everything. "You see, I own a ton of restored cars. Hard-to-find classics that I pay a ton of money to restore. I believe you'd make an excellent contact for my car obsession."

She pointed to the 916. "I'm flattered, and I enjoy a challenge."

Bradly removed his jacket and looked at several surfaces, and then he decided to put it back on and roll up the sleeves. "Then let's take a look." He popped the hood and joined her at the front of the car.

"I do my best work with the radio cranked and no one watching. How about I do a full assessment and meet up with you later with an itemized list of what needs to be done?"

He looked at his watch. "Glad to hear it. I've got to run. My car should be outside waiting on me now. I'll be in touch soon." He bolted from the garage as if he worried his suit would be tainted by simply being near the grease.

She loved the car and the opportunity to work on it, so that's what she focused on for hours. Her music blared and she found her rhythm. She was so lost in her zone that she never heard anyone call her or open the door.

Not until the music cut off and she shot up, hitting her head on the hood. A sharp pain shot down her neck. "Ouch."

"Are you okay?" Knox was at her side. "I called out and you never answered. I didn't want to startle you, so I turned off the music.

She pressed her fingers to the edge of her hairline to discover blood. It throbbed in protest.

"Oh damn... Here. Sit down." Knox grabbed one of her lawn chairs and eased her into it. "Do you feel dizzy?"

"No. I'm fine. Seriously." Stella went to stand, but Knox

nudged her back. "Let me get a clean rag for you." He raced out of sight.

"What are you doing here?" Stella asked—but not too loud since her head ached.

"I thought I'd offer to take you out to dinner. This time it won't be to a steak place, I promise."

"You mean you came to check up on me," Stella grumbled. "You want me to put aside this car and work on your show."

Knox knelt in front of her and gently pressed a damp paper towel to the cut on her head. The man was attentive and kind, a juxtaposition from the man on the Internet.

He chuckled. "Yes, but that's not why I'm here. I just wanted to apologize one more time for what happened with Lori's research. You know you didn't do anything wrong." The way he looked at her, touched her, leaned into her, promised comfort and hope. Something she couldn't afford to believe. Not from him. Not from any man. She rested back against the chair to put space between them. It wasn't because he made her feel uncomfortable but because he didn't that made her want to run.

"It's none of your business, and I don't need you digging up things that are best left in the past. As for dinner, I can't." A part of her wanted to abandon her work for dinner, but what did Knox offer except the promise of embarrassment on an international level? Now she understood why Carissa had been so reluctant to be in the first segment. The vulnerability of calling attention to herself and the world wanting to know more about her drove her to want to live under the car hood.

"I know you're mad, but—"

"I'm not mad."

He stood and hovered over her, blowing warm air over her cut, soothing the ache. She'd never felt so cared for before. Her father had always told her to stop crying and rub dirt on it. Her skin warmed and her face flushed, but it was the want of his lips pressed to her skin that made her bolt. "I don't trust you, but that isn't the point. I have plans tonight."

Knox folded the red-stained paper towel in half. "Oh. I understand."

"What, you don't think I have plans?" Stella's hackles rose, despite his soft eyes and touch.

"I only meant that I was disappointed because I'd hoped to take you out tonight." He looked vulnerable, open to knowing her better, humbled.

Her shoulders lowered, and so did her shield. The shield that had protected her from every man who had entered her life since she was thirteen. And at that moment, she'd never been so scared in her life.

EIGHTEEN

Knox didn't want to return to the office and have to deal with Lori's questions or to the inn where he'd probably find Carissa and Drew snuggling on the front porch swing having a picnic lunch. He'd love to find the closest bar, but in Sugar Maple the strongest thing he could have was an espresso. He headed for a quiet cup of coffee at Maple Grounds, far from everyone.

To his disappointment, the senior bus pulled up outside and out shuffled five town elders, Davey leading the pack. "What you lookin' so glum for? A squirrel steal your teeth?" Davey plopped down across from Knox as if he had been invited. "Don't look at me like I'm crazy. It happened once. Squirrel ran right up on my porch, grabbed my teeth, and skittered away."

The man was like comedic relief for Knox's gloomy life, but he didn't want the entertainment right then. Knox thought about asking why he'd left his teeth on an outside porch but decided that would only open up more conversation.

"So what is it? Girl trouble?" Davey pushed his bony elbow into Knox's bicep.

Knox snugged his coffee closer to him, cupping it like a life raft. "It's nothing."

"Nothin' wouldn't have you looking like Eeyore just lost Pooh in the woods."

Another town elder approached. He'd learned never to call them anything but elders after sweet tea was poured over his head for saying geriatrics. "Is this a private chat, or can I join you?" Mrs. Malter, the tea-pouring lady, sat down before anyone could answer.

"Sure, we were just talking about him yearning for a girl."

"You mean Jacqueline?" Mrs. Malter covered her mouth with oversized round knuckles.

Davey grunted. "You're behind on town news. How do I know more than you?"

Knox took a long gulp from his coffee, downing it as fast as he could instead of savoring it.

"Who, then?" Mrs. Malter dropped her hands to the table and smiled scary wide. The woman had big teeth.

"Stella," Davey said with the movement of a mechanical circus ringmaster who needed oiling of his joints.

"No!" Melba came over, and Knox looked to the door, but before he had a chance to make his escape, the woman put her hand around his arm in a vise grip. The old people in Sugar Maple were eerily strong.

Knox managed to slip his phone from his pocket under the table and text Lori since the elders were too busy arguing over his love life to notice. He knew better than to insult them or he'd pay a great price. No way he'd get tar and southernized like Drew had done voluntarily. The vision of him walking into the town square with leaves and maple syrup covering him still haunted Knox.

"So who is it?" Davey smacked his hand to the tabletop.

Knox thought about lying or telling them that he indeed thought Stella was interesting, but he only shook his head.

"Care to make a wager? I'll put a twenty that says it's Jacqueline." Mrs. Malter rapped her knuckles on the tabletop.

"I'll put fifty down that it's Mary-Beth." The other woman, Ms. Gina, knocked on the table. Davey and Melba looked at the blue-haired woman like the dye had gone to her brain. "Why else would he always be in the coffee shop?" She laughed with a hen cackle.

"I'll take that fifty." Davey rapped on the table and smiled like a gambling addict about to score his big win. "I put it on Stella."

They all looked to Knox to confirm or deny, but he didn't answer.

Melba scooted her chair out. "Well, doesn't matter. I win."

"How you figure that?" Davey asked.

Melba's facial lines deepened from an oversized smile. "Because Jacqueline was overheard saying she didn't like Knox, and we all know Mary-Beth and Knox would never happen."

The group of elders nodded their agreement.

"That mean's I win. It's Stella." Davey declared.

"I can prove it's not Stella," Melba said with an air of superiority.

"How's that?" Mrs. Malter asked.

"Because she's on a date with another man right now." Melba pointed her finger at the front window, and sure enough, Stella walked side by side with Bradley.

Knox's gut burned. His muscles tightened. The simple world of Sugar Maple turned on its side. He didn't know why, but he needed to interject himself between those two. Knox abandoned the geriatric crew and headed outside.

Drew and Lori walked up laughing until they saw him. Drew blocked Knox's view of Stella. "Don't do it, soldier."

"Stand down. I can't let my chance at a show be destroyed by a beautiful woman." Knox fisted his hands.

"So you admit she's beautiful." Drew's lip curled into a gotcha grin.

Lori inserted herself between Drew and Knox. "Don't you have to go meet Carissa? I need Knox here to take a walk with me."

Knox didn't move.

A steady breeze made the new green leaves shake the way he wanted to shake Stella until she saw the truth about the man. Lori slid her hand into the crook of his elbow.

Drew stood down but kept an eye on Knox. "I don't know why he's with her right now, but I know they aren't supposed to go out until dinner."

"Dinner?"

"A meal to talk about the car restoration. They are in business together, remember?"

Knox rubbed his scalp, the heated, anxious feeling driving him to want to do something stupid, like ask Stella out on a real date. "I guess this means she's going to pass on my show, then."

"You marching over there will only make things worse." Lori yanked him, this time until his feet moved in the direction she wanted him to follow.

"Don't let them out of your sight," Knox ordered, as if Drew still had to follow his commands.

"I'm on it." Drew saluted and jogged to the corner Stella had disappeared around.

Knox followed Lori in the opposite direction. He was losing it and needed to get a grip before he blew everything. In the past, he'd focus on controlling the situation and bending people to do what he needed, but Stella didn't bend. "I'm not sure this guy is ever going to follow through on my show."

"You're worried that he's wasting your time and he's going put all his attention into his car and Stella."

He halted. "Don't you even care? Bradley stated he wanted the car show if I wanted to sign that contract. That's what you told me. And I can't get five minutes with him to discuss our options. All of our hard work is going to be for nothing if we don't get a grip on this."

"You worry too much." Lori stepped back and took a breath. "You really like Stella, don't you?"

He ran a hand through his hair and walked down the sidewalk toward the office. "That's not what this is about."

They walked in silence, and Knox realized denying it to himself was one thing, but Lori already knew what was in his heart. "More than I should."

"Why?" Lori caught up to him. "You can't protect yourself forever."

He reached the old building turned temporary office and wrenched the door open. The smell of musty old walls and over-stained hardwood floors welcomed him inside. "She's not interested. If she were, she wouldn't be with Bradley."

The door slammed behind them. He walked past the old shop turned recreation center for the elders turned empty space and headed up the old creaky stairs.

"She's not into him at all. I've seen the way she looks at you. Trust me, if she's into anyone, it would be you." Lori flipped on the light to reveal green paint peeling from the corner and the smell of day-old coffee.

"You should try to go spend some time with her, show her that you're trustworthy." Lori plopped down on the couch and propped her feet up on the old coffee table. "What you don't want to do is turn into controlling, combative Knox."

He sat in the chair behind his desk and grabbed the little green man stress ball. "I already proved she could trust me. I found out what the mug shot was for, and I promised not to tell anyone. She opened up to me and I thought we connected, but then she pushed me away."

"Why should she trust you?" Lori asked.

Knox squeezed the stress ball, watching the eyes bubble between his fingers. "I told her to. What else can I do?"

Lori sighed and dropped her feet to the ground. "A girl as strong as Stella doesn't open up to a guy easily."

"She didn't mean to. She thought I knew the truth." He released his grip and squeezed again.

"So she spilled her guts and then you opened up to her, right?" Lori did that judgmental, I-know-you-blew-it expression.

He blinked at her. "What?"

"You told her about something that happened in your life?" Lori sat on the edge of the desk. "I know you don't want to talk about it, but you need to tell Stella why you're distant and closed off to her."

A prick of warning at the direction of their conversation made his jaw twitch. "I'm not. I told you that we talked and I told her she could trust me."

"Words are empty promises that are usually broken. Think about it. Would you want to be around Stella if she knew the truth about what happened to you in Iraq, and then she promised to keep it a secret? You wouldn't feel comfortable. You'd feel like she knew too much. You'd feel vulnerable, and you wouldn't like it. I'm guessing that Stella is a lot like you and she doesn't want to see you because of how exposed she feels when you're around."

"That's ridiculous." He tossed the stress ball against the wall and caught it.

"Really? Think about it. Bradley's easy, a business relationship. One she can hide behind to focus on what she does best: hiding under a car."

"Yeah, so?" He tossed the ball against the wall again, but Lori caught it this time.

"Remind you of anyone we know?" She looked down at him. "Pours himself into work and avoids any real connections with people to keep from feeling any real pain?"

NINETEEN

Stella eyed the ticking time bomb clock. Only ten more minutes until she escaped from wedding planning torture and into a free dinner to discuss cars.

"Don't twist the tulle that way." Jackie grabbed the white netting from her hands. "You do it this way. In the shape of a rosebud."

Carissa rolled her eyes and knotted the fabric into a big puffy ball. "Like this?"

Jackie dropped the perfect rose shape into Stella's lap. "No! Look at Felicia's."

Felicia shrugged. "Flowers are my thing, remember?"

"Okay, Mrs. Switzerland," Stella snipped.

"What's up with you tonight? You're more sassy than normal." Mary-Beth abandoned her attempt at a flower on the table and scooted to the edge of her seat. "I heard that you and Mr. Bradley walked here together. How will Knox feel about that?"

Stella tore the fabric. "Oops."

Jackie shot an angry stare over her shoulder. "You did that on purpose, knowing I would do it for you if you messed up."

"I didn't think of that. But now that you say it..." Stella smiled like an innocent child.

Jackie snatched the ripped tulle from her hands. "Give me that. You're all hopeless. Fine, you can go, but on Friday you will help finish the centerpieces."

"You do know that the wedding is over six months from now."

"I know, and there's so much more to do." Jackie untwisted Stella's fabric and set it in the large wicker basket.

Mary-Beth placed hers in the basket and then sat next to Stella. "So, what's the scoop? You courting Bradley now? Knox out, Bradley in?"

"Courting? What are you? Sixty years old?" Stella snagged her jacket, despite the warming temperatures. "No one is in."

"Oh no, you don't. Where are you off to so fast?" Carissa sidestepped in front of Stella. "We want to know what's going on. We don't know this man and don't know if we approve of you dating him."

"I'm not dating him." Stella gnawed on the inside of her cheek.

Before she could escape, there was a circle of four around her, Carissa in front and the rest at her sides and back. "You guys about to chant or something? I feel like I'm in a witches' circle about to be turned into a toad."

"No toad." Felicia leaned around her shoulder and tapped Stella's nose. "But I think that's growing. You a cousin of Pinocchio's?"

She swatted Felicia's hand out of her face. "No date. No lies. No need to approve."

The friend circle didn't budge.

"Why are you dressed up today?" Jackie asked her from behind.

"I'm not. I'm in jeans and my jacket like usual."

Mary-Beth joined the interrogation. "Your nice jeans. The ones you only wear when you're going out to eat or to a movie."

Carissa adjusted Stella's jacket. "Are you going to meet Bradley for dinner? I mean, he escorted you here and everything."

"He didn't escort me. He was walking this way, so we walked together." Stella slid between Carissa and Mary-Beth and managed to reach the door. She didn't like the interrogation about Bradley, but it was safer than answering questions about Knox. The man who kept her up all night with confusing dreams and thinking about what ifs that would never be. The man who knew too much. She was ready for him to leave town, but at the same time she wanted him to stay.

Life sucked.

"Don't do anything I wouldn't do to win a rich producer's attention," Jackie said in a sexy tone.

"I'd never resort to your level to get what I want." Stella burst through the door to escape the friendship fire ring. Of course, she should have just told them the truth since they'd know thirty seconds after she sat down inside the diner with Bradley to discuss the car.

The senior bus parked outside Maple Table and the screech of the lift lowering made Stella stop short of the front door. No. It was Wednesday, but the seniors were always done eating by five and on the bus by five thirty. Davey shuffled up to the door and tried to open it for Stella, but he only fell into it.

"Let me get that," Stella said. "Hey, isn't it like...bedtime for all the elders?"

Davey tipped his Cuban-looking hat at her. "Yep, but the bus driver couldn't get the lift to work, so we couldn't go since Mr. Parker's gout is acting up and he can't climb the stairs. What are you doing here?"

"Business meeting."

Davy half danced through the door. "Is that what the young people are calling it these days?"

Trapped holding the door open for the elders who moved slower than a slug on valium, she had to stand there and listen to Davey.

"You know, in my day, I'd pick the young woman up at her front door. The men who didn't were not the kind a woman should be out with. I remember a boy honking his horn to take my sister out—me and my brother went out and taught him how to be a gentleman."

"I guess the boy was more respectful after that." Stella managed to escape when a gentleman took the door from her.

"Nope. He never showed up at our house again. Apparently we ruined our sister's dating life and no boy would ask her out after that." Davey hiked up his highwater brown pants and took Melba by the arm. "This way, my dear. I ordered the best table in the house just for you."

Stella spotted Bradley already sitting at the table dead center of the diner. He looked like he worried about small-town contamination with his hands resting on his thighs and his posture straighter than Mrs. Malter's walker. Great... She'd made the mistake of looking under the 916's hood and falling in love with the project before she technically had it. She needed to keep Bradley from running from Sugar Maple before they reached an agreement.

"I know I'm a couple minutes late. I won't be on the car restoration. Today was unique since we were wedding planning for the mayor and it took longer than I'd thought."

He bolted to his feet and pulled her chair out for her, as if he knew Davey would be watching and scoring his manners. "You sure you don't want me to take you somewhere more...quiet?"

The elders crowded around a long table, and two of them

picked up a fork and knife and pounded them against the table, chanting, "We want our food. We want our food."

"They weren't supposed to eat at this time. They eat at five o'clock, but we're here now. Unfortunately, this is it for Sugar Maple dining that I'd be willing to eat at. We'll have to make do."

Bradley tucked her under the table and then lifted his hand like he was summoning a wine sommelier to order some expensive Cabernet.

The waitress shot by. "Just a sec, you two. I'll be right back. The natives are restless." She went and plopped some sodas onto the elders' table and removed her pad and pen.

"Best settle in," Bradley said apathetically. "Looks like we aren't her priority at the moment."

Considering she was facing the town elders with a late dinner, he had a point. And knowing she didn't want Bradley witnessing Davey with low blood sugar, Stella unrolled the silverware and placed the napkin in her lap. "She's trying to keep the peace so that we don't suffer. We can discuss the 916 while we wait, though."

Bradly nodded. "That's why we're here. Shoot."

"I've finished the list, and I'll email it to you as soon as I return to the garage." With her hands hidden under the table so he couldn't see her picking at her nails like she always did when she was nervous, she said a silent prayer that the man would agree for her to do the work. She needed the money, and she needed it now. So, she took in a deep breath and spilled the grand total on him. "It'll cost around twenty thousand to fully restore the 916 into a show car. That's with everything vintage like we discussed. I've priced the parts out, and it really is the least expensive you can manage with a serious discount on labor."

She held her breath. This could be her way out of all this.

To concentrate on the car and forget the show. She'd calculated the labor costs to the penny of what she needed to keep her shop from being torn down.

"Okay."

Stella blinked at him. "Okay so you want me to send you the list to look over?"

"No. I already knew how much it would cost. I know what I'm doing. I don't make mistakes," Bradley said in an authoritative tone.

She let out a long breath. "Okay, so..."

"So get to work." Bradley eyed the waitress, as if deciding business was concluded and maybe the meal wasn't necessary. "To be honest, you came in seven thousand less than my guy."

Her breath caught, knowing she had to push a little further with the next question she had no choice but to ask. "Can I get half the money prior to starting and half when the job is done?"

"I usually pay at the end," he said in a light tone, as if ten thousand was of little significance to him.

She fisted her hands under the table, willing him to agree, and said the next thing she'd rehearsed in the mirror last night. "Then you'll have to work with your other guy. You see, I don't overcharge, which means I need the money so that I can order all the parts and keep the lights on while I work."

He let out a long huff, showing his patience was thinning at the lack of service. "Fine. Email me your bank routing and account numbers, and I'll make the transfer tonight."

"What can I get ya both?" The waitress had better timing than Mayor Horton attending to town business.

"I'll have the chicken with potatoes, and the lady will have the same."

The waitress chuckled. "The usual, Stella?"

"Yes, the *lady* will have the usual." Stella slid her chair an inch away from Bradley.

Bradley swirled his ice around in his water. "A woman who knows what she wants. I can respect that. I can see why Knox is less focused on his show and more on you."

Stella snagged her water and downed a few gulps. "You've got it wrong. There's nothing between Knox and me. I'm just not interested in fame and fortune. His show is the last thing I want to do, yet the town needs me to agree."

"I'll be honest. If you don't do the show, I'm going to push Knox back until this Sugar Maple series ends and I see how his ratings stand. The only reason I was interested now was because I knew a car show would redeem him from his fiasco from before. Once his image is fully restored, the network will make him an offer."

"So his future is determined by my decision?"

"I'm afraid it is, but you need to do what's best for you," Bradley said, as if discussing the weather, not the fact that she held a man's hopes and dreams in her hands.

She downed the rest of the water and smacked the empty glass down on the table in hopes the waitress would run over and refill it, but unfortunately the elders had her busy. She'd never felt so alone around so many people before. "I will think about it more and give him and you an answer soon."

"You have three days. I'll be leaving to attend to business back in LA and will return to check on my car and your answer when I'm done."

Stella nodded mutely, unsure what to say.

"Then our business is concluded. I have my jet waiting, so I need to head out." Bradley lifted his hand to order the waitress over. "Check please."

She halted near their table with a tray full of glasses resting on her shoulder. "You haven't had anything but water." The waitress slid her pad from her pocket and shrugged. "Nothing to charge you for, but feel free to leave a tip."

"So you won't pull the show until you return?" Stella asked, her pulse hammering against her neck.

"I don't make promises until a contract is signed. There are many options and directions I can choose for my next season."

Bradley headed for the door, and that's when Stella realized what she'd done. She hadn't only jeopardized Knox's future, but that of Sugar Maple. That of her best friends, who counted on her so they would have their turn to show off their businesses. How could Stella look at herself in the mirror if Felicia lost her nursery or even if Jackie lost her dress store?

A knot of indecision tightened her gut. Maybe she could work with Knox on the car restoration show and forget her own wants and needs to avoid the world of fame she despised so much for the sake of the town.

Maybe.

TWENTY

Knox walked up the street mumbling to himself. "Stella, I realize how vulnerable you must've felt." He threw his hands up in the air. Great. Lori had him talking to himself now. He was two steps from crazy.

This was ridiculous. Why did he have to open some gaping wound to talk to Stella? He could just tell her he understood and that he'd had some bad things happen to him that he didn't want to talk about. That should be enough. She either liked him or she didn't. He couldn't force her. Still, if she chose Bradley's car offer over his show, he couldn't be with her. So what if she didn't want fame? She was tough enough to handle the attention. Wasn't she? Was it all an act? No woman could be that tough.

He'd made a mistake believing that about Alima, and that hadn't ended well at all.

In the distance, he saw a couple pressed up against the side wall of the diner. As he neared, he knew the woman to be Stella and the shmuck getting handsy was Bradley. He hotfooted it toward them. When he was within earshot, he heard them talking, so he stopped to listen.

The streetlight cut on between them, so he sidestepped into the nearby doorway of the closed art store.

Bradley moved in closer.

Stella pressed her back against the wall. "You'll wire me the money in the morning, right?"

Knox saw red. He stepped out into the light and got ready to charge if the man didn't move. "Get your hands off her. Just because you're a big-time producer doesn't mean you have the right to make advances toward every woman you meet. She's an employee, not your plaything." He fisted his hands. "She can't be bought like a prostitute."

Stella shoved past Bradley and marched to Knox. "How dare you! I'm not a prostitute. I can't believe you."

Knox realized what he'd said and how it sounded. "I didn't mean that. I just meant that you don't have to make this guy happy to get what you want. You're too good for that kind of game."

"May I remind you that your show also rests in my hands? And I'm not sure I want to work with a man who treats a lady like that." Bradley placed a hand on Stella's shoulder, as if to claim her as his. "You should apologize to the lady for calling her a prostitute."

"I didn't call her that. I only meant..." Knox shook his head. "Why did you have her cornered?"

Stella went nose-to-chin with Knox. "Not that I owe you an explanation, but I didn't eat all day and I drank champagne earlier with the girls, so when we came outside I was dizzy and had to lean on the wall for a moment." She whirled around, flipping hair into Knox's eyes.

She offered her hand to Bradley, as if confirming a business transaction. "Thank you for your time."

Bradley caught her elbow. "I'll take you home."

"No need. The fresh air will do me good. Besides, I need to

stop by Carissa's. I don't know how long I'll be. For now, since I don't have a vested interest in the show any longer, I'm going to leave you two television gurus to discuss the future of streaming shows. Good night." Stella nodded to Bradley, looked at Knox with a snarl, and hotfooted it away.

Knox went after her, but Bradley shot his arm out in front of him. "I think it'd be best if you gave her some space. It's up to her at this moment if your show is going to continue. You have a few days to make this right with Stella, or I'm pulling the plug for now and we'll reevaluate next season."

"That's your decision to make." Knox pushed back his shoulders. "You don't know the backstory on what just happened, and I respect Stella too much to share, but what I saw was a man who appeared to be cornering a woman, and I did what I thought was right."

"Fight. Fight," Davey shouted from the diner doorway. "Knock-Out Knox defending Stella's honor."

Knox stepped back before he provided the entertainment to all of Sugar Maple, knowing fighting Bradley was the last thing that would win Stella over. "Sorry to disappoint there, Davey. We're just having a conversation. You best get back inside before you catch cold in this damp air."

"You knock him out, and we'll tar and southernize him," Davey yelled.

Knox chuckled at the idea. Was that what it would take to prove himself to Stella? God, he hoped not. "Stand down."

Bradley's expression softened. "Listen, I get it. You like Stella, and you were looking out for her. But I need to give you a piece of advice. That woman doesn't need protection. She needs someone who believes in her and will stand by her side. If you care for her the way you appear to and she is worth the risk of your show and heart, lose the attitude and tell her how you feel."

Knox didn't respond to Bradley, but his words did register. And the scary realization was that yes, she was worth it. But could he do what it took to get her to trust him? Could he tell her the one thing he'd never said aloud, not even to himself?

TWENTY-ONE

"Jake. Don't you cower from me. No need. I've got your money for rent and then some."

Stella stomped up the front steps. A red cardinal hanging on the birdfeeder at the edge of the porch took off. Spring brought new life and new hope into the world.

A click of the lock sounded, and the door creaked open only far enough for her to see Jake's brown eyes and red patch of hair sprouting at the front like a bad hair plug. "Give it to me, then." A pasty white hand shot out from the door with fingers outstretched and palm up, waiting.

"I don't have it yet, but it's supposed to be in my bank this morning. I've landed a major car restoration project."

The door creaked open enough to reveal dark circles under his eyes and sunken-in cheeks. She'd always thought he ducked inside to hide from her because she scared him, but in that moment she saw more than just fear. "Dude, come out here in the sun. Why are you always inside?"

The door opened a little farther. "No need. I've got everything I need here."

Stella edged closer, but it sent Jake back a few steps. "I'm headed over to Maple Grounds. You want to walk with me? Looks like you could use some fresh air and sunshine."

The door slammed shut. "No, just bring the money today."

Stella heard his retreating steps. How had she never noticed Jake's suffering? Because she'd been so caught up in her own. She left, but the image of him followed her up the street and into the town square. Jake had lost his mother a year ago. Had he been locked inside that house all that time? Was he depressed like Stella had been after her *abuelo* died?

"Good morning. How are things going for the show?" Ms. Horton put her arm around Stella and walked by her side, despite the fact that she already held a coffee in her hand.

"Don't know about the show." Stella looked at her feet, shame filling her. She should've agreed to do the show. Why couldn't she just do it for the town and forget her own selfish needs?

"Really? I've been doing some digging into Knox, and he's not such a bad guy. Did you know he donates ten percent of his income to the Oscar Mike foundation for wounded veterans?"

"Knox does that? The same Knox who cares only about himself and what he can get out of everyone around him?"

Stella's words weren't lost on herself. Had she treated Jake the way Knox treated everyone else? "Hey, what's Jake's deal?"

"Jake Shoemaker?"

"Yeah."

Ms. Horton sighed. "I'm afraid he's been struggling for a while now. He suffers from a condition called agoraphobia."

Stella put her arm out to stop Ms. Horton from stepping into the street as a rogue car barreled through town. "Watch it!" she shouted at the stupid outsider threatening her town. "But he used to go outside all the time. I remember him playing his guitar at the town fair a few years ago. He was good."

"Yes, but his mother was around then to help him overcome

his challenges. She would monitor his antidepressant and make sure he attended therapy. I'm afraid that no one can get him out of the house now that his mother has passed."

They stepped up to the front walk of Maple Grounds. "That's awful. What can I do?"

Ms. Horton blinked at her and tilted her head.

"What?" Stella asked, knowing that look of confusion.

"Nothing."

"Are you saying I don't care about anyone but myself?" Stella didn't want to hear the answer but knew she needed to face it all at the same time.

"No, dear. It's just that I'm surprised you didn't knock down his door and drag him out."

Stella shrugged. "I can pull him out, but he'd only run back inside."

"True. I guess the only way we can support him is to try to let him know we all care about him without overwhelming him. I've tried, but I think he sees his mother every time I go to his door."

"Kindness, huh?" Stella eyed the coffee shop. "Okay, I'll try." She paused before opening the door to the café. "Um, what if the show doesn't work out?"

"I heard about the incident outside the diner last night." Ms. Horton's lips pursed into a thin line of disapproval. "You know the elders were there, so the entire town knows."

"Yep. I saw them." Stella sighed. "I tried, I really did. Listen, I didn't even slug Knox when he showed up, ordering me around."

"Knox?" Ms. Horton rubbed her arm as if to calm the brewing storm that raged inside Stella. "From what I heard, I think for once you should've slugged him."

Stella stepped from Ms. Horton, feeling guilty for not trying harder to make the show with Knox work. She had to make a decision, but for now, she could concentrate on working on the Porsche 916 as soon as the money cleared her bank. She slid her phone from her pocket and checked. Nope. No money yet.

She couldn't buy any parts until the money came through, so she went to the register and snapped her fingers to get Mary-Beth's attention from the other side of the counter. "I need two drinks. My usual and another one, but I don't know what to order."

"I know the perfect drink for Knox."

"It's not for Knox." What was people's obsession about Knox all about? "I need one for Jake Shoemaker."

Mary-Beth's jaw dropped as fast as the pen from her hand hit the floor. "I'm not going to be a part of you drawing Jake out so you can intimidate him over your rent."

Stella studied the oil under her fingernails. "I deserve that I guess. That's your one comment, though. I'm not going to do that. I want to take it to him in hopes it might cheer him up. He doesn't look so good."

"Oh no. I haven't seen him in months. I know the perfect drink." Mary-Beth set to working her barista magic.

Stella dared another look at her bank app. Still only twenty-two dollars left in her checking account. How could she have been so naïve? She'd chased off Knox, who promised a long road to increase her business, so she could take the quick cut-through instead.

There was nothing she could do right now. Considering Jake's state, she couldn't ask for an extension on rent. Instead, she could focus on helping him instead of bullying him. She'd cleared her entire day to work on the 916, but that obviously wasn't going to happen, so she texted Felicia.

Could you bring some inexpensive plants to Jake Shoemaker's house? His mother's flowered looks terrible, and he isn't doing so well.

The espresso machine squealed, letting Stella know it wouldn't be long now.

Have the perfect plants. I'll load them in the truck and meet you at Jake's place.

Jackie sauntered into the café for her morning cup. "Hello, ladies. I hear congratulations are in order. Stella has two men fighting over her." She hiked her handbag up her arm and looked down her nose at Stella. "Although, I can't imagine why."

Stella was tired. Tired of fighting. Tired of being angry. Tired of being alone. Instead of tossing back an insult, she straightened to her full height, even if it was several inches shorter than Jackie in her six-inch heels. "I call a Fabulous Five Intervention."

Mary-Beth and Jackie both gasped.

"You've never called a Fabulous Five Intervention. What's wrong?" Mary-Beth fidgeted with her five gold bracelets clanking against the counter. How that woman worked with so much jewelry, Stella could never understand. "Nothing with me. I can't call a Fabulous Five Intervention on myself. That's against the rules."

"I didn't know that you ever listened to the rules." Jackie's tone unnervingly softened. "Who are you calling it for, then?"

"For Jake."

"Pasty Jake?" Jackie's eyebrows knitted together.

"Jake Shoemaker. He's one of our own from Sugar Maple, and we don't turn our back on anyone. Well, not anymore."

"This is some sort of trick. I'm not falling for it." Jackie set her bag on the counter and placed her hands on her hips.

"It's not. I saw him this morning, and he's in bad shape. I feel responsible, and I want to help him. I don't know how yet, but Felicia is bringing plants and meeting me at his house in a bit. Mary-Beth made him some coffee. I'm not sure what else we can do."

"Does this meet the requirements for an intervention?" Mary-Beth asked. "What's the critical need?"

"He's depressed and mentally unwell. Not to mention he appears to be deteriorating physically."

"That's solid," Jackie said with a steady nod.

Mary-Beth patted her hand. "Don't worry. We'll help."

Jackie shrugged. "I don't have a choice. You called it, and it fits the guidelines."

Stella took in a deep breath of cinnamon and espresso–scented air. "Now what?"

"What do you mean?" Mary-Beth asked.

Stella shrugged. "I don't know what I'm supposed to do next. I've never called one of these before."

For a second, Stella thought she saw a glimmer of happiness from Jackie, as if Stella calling this meant something to her. "I'll head over to the bakery and talk to Carissa about supplying some goodies for him. Then I'll meet with the town elders." She clicked away without even ordering her coffee. Maybe Jackie really did want to make amends so they could return to being a friend-family again.

"What can I do?" Mary-Beth asked.

Stella snagged the two cups waiting for her on the counter. "If Knox comes in here, make him the most perfect cup of coffee."

"Really?" Mary-Beth narrowed her eyes.

"Yeah, and then spit in it." Stella stomped away.

"That's the Stella we know and love. Don't take any prisoners, girl!"

TWENTY-TWO

Sugar Maple roared to life as if spring sprouted the town's activity. Felicia drove by in her old truck full of plants with a sideways wave.

Knox stood at the corner next to Maple Grounds, watching the people head up the hill toward Stella's side of town. Intrigue nipped at him.

Despite the fact he'd already enjoyed his morning coffee, he headed inside to purchase a cup along with some information. "Hi, Mary-Beth. How's it going?"

"Good, I'm glad you're here." Mary-Beth rounded the counter holding a drink carrier with five drinks. "Could you drop this at Jake's place? I have one for Stella, too, even though she just took some with her. I figured she could use an extra today. I'd go, but I still have a few customers. Let Stella know that I'll close up shop for lunch and be there to help."

"Help with what?" Knox caught a whiff of almond and knew that had to be for Drew.

"The town is helping shake Jake Shoemaker out of his grief and step outside to enjoy some fresh air."

"I don't follow." Knox took the tray of coffee and rested it on the counter. "It looks like there's something major going on up the hill. Everything okay at Stella's place?"

"Yep, she's good. It's a Fabulous Five Intervention called by Stella herself."

He knew this had to be big news, the way Mary-Beth twirled her bracelets around her wrist and stood on her toes. The girl was animated when excited.

"I see you're not following." She wiggled her wrist so that the bracelets went higher on her arm and then put her hand up with five fingers splayed apart. "When a Fabulous Five Intervention is called, the town listens. It's been over a decade since one has been ordered, and Stella's never called one. Ever."

His stomach twisted with concern. "Is she okay?"

"What?" She waved her hands in front of her face. "Yes. She didn't call it for herself. That isn't allowed. She'd never do that. Not our Stella. Heck, she'd never ask for help even if she was drowning in the lake with a fifty-pound weight attached to her ankle."

"That's accurate. Then who did she call it for?"

"I told you. To bring Jake out of his house. He lost his mother, and his agoraphobia is worse. The town wants to help him."

"The entire town cares about one person who doesn't want to leave his house? Is he sick?"

"In a way. I guess inside he is, with the loss of his mama and all."

Knox scratched his head. "There are a ton of people. Looks like almost the entire town headed that way."

"Yep. So you better get moving. I heard Drew didn't have time for coffee this morning because of some big order Carissa had to fill. We're gonna have to call in some help if they ever hope to have some time together outside of that bakery."

She grabbed a towel and shooed him away. Well, at least

he'd have an excuse to talk to Stella again. Not that he'd confess his darkest secrets in front of the entire town, but maybe he'd earn some brownie points for bringing coffee.

He set off up the hill, finding himself smiling back at strangers-turned-acquaintances over the past month or so he'd been staying in Sugar Maple. The innkeeper hobbled up the hill ahead, the corner store owner, along with the receptionist to the mayor, and Maple Table's owner turned left down a side street before they reached Stella's garage. He figured this had to be the way, so he followed along with the crowd.

Only a few hundred feet down the road, he spotted Felicia's nursery truck, with Drew standing a few feet away, waving at him.

Knox zigzagged through the people.

"You brought coffee?" Drew grabbed the cup closest to him, setting the carrier off-center, but Knox managed to keep the remaining four upright. Drew took a sip and then handed it to Carissa, who brushed off her work overalls and took it from him.

"Thanks for joining us. We hope to be done in the next few hours with everyone chipping in to help."

"Why's Stella doing this?" Knox asked.

Carissa lowered the cup from her lips and smiled. "I think she felt bad. With her owing him so much money to keep her grandfather's garage, I think she might have been less than friendly attempting to persuade him into giving her more time to pay the rent. When she found out what Jake was going through, I think she wanted to make it up to him."

"She's going to lose her garage?"

Carissa blinked at him. "You didn't know? Of course you didn't. Would you mind not telling Stella that I told you? Between you and me, she's my best friend, but I'm still a little scared of her at times."

Drew wrapped his arm around Carissa's shoulder. "We all

are. She's one tough lady."

How could one woman be this strong? If Alima had been, she'd be alive today. If only he had convinced her to leave her family and small-town prejudice for the larger city, she'd be alive.

"You okay?" Carissa reached for him, but he shook off the electricity shooting through him, stealing his breath, and retreated.

"I'm good." He broke free of their concerned stares and took advantage of the twenty paces up the front lawn to the flowerbed to regain his composure. How did memories still threaten to take him down without warning? Even the whiz of a bullet or the whoosh of a rocket indicated danger approaching. Remembering tragic events had no caution signs.

Stella crouched, digging a hole, with flowers stacked around her. The sight of her calmed his inner panic. He'd never had the sting on his skin or the tightness in his chest fade so quickly. Her strength confounded him. The way she faced her past without letting it cripple her and still appear strong enough to hold others up around her confounded him.

He dodged a man carrying two rakes and hopped over a small bush in a planter. He stood at the edge of the flowerbed watching her dig and toss the soil to the side.

Stella impaled the ground with her hand shovel, brushed her hands down her overalls, and stood. "You gonna stand there all day, or are you here to help?" She grabbed one of the three remaining coffees and took a sip.

That wasn't what he was expecting. Yelling at him and kicking him off the property or throwing dirt at him maybe. But a half-invitation to stay? He'd take it. "Oh, um, sure. I can help." He held up the last two coffees sitting in the carrier. "I just need to deliver these to whomever ordered them. I see the one says Jake on it. I don't know who the other one is for."

"It's for me." Stella held out the cup she'd drunk from. "And this must be yours."

"I didn't order—"

"Didn't have to, but now I've got an idea of what you like. Mary-Beth only creates the perfect beverage for a person. Although, I don't know what I drank. Was that cloves?"

"Something like that."

They traded coffees, and he set the tray on the ground nearby. "Tell me what to do."

"Go up to the front door, ring the bell, and leave the coffee. At some point, Jake will open to get it. Don't stand there, though. He'll never come out if you do."

Knox did as instructed, but the door didn't open even when he reached the bottom of the stairs. "Okay, what's next? You want me to dig?"

"I was only joking. I don't expect the famous Knox Brevard to get his hands dirty." She squatted and retrieved her shovel.

No way he'd allow any more distance between them. She held his life in her hands, and he wasn't about to give up. He knelt by her side, not caring that his khaki pants were going to have permanent red clay knee stains on them. There would be a chance to buy new clothes, but he wasn't sure there'd be another opportunity to get some semi-alone time with Stella.

A woman walked by and dropped another hand shovel into a bucket, so he retrieved it and began digging. "You know, this is a good thing you're doing here."

She didn't say anything. Obviously he had to dig deeper than small talk. He wanted to offer to pay for the plants or therapy for this Jake person, but he knew better than to play financial hero. "It takes a special kind of person to help someone who threatens their dreams."

"Who told you? Mary-Beth? She's going to be wearing the next cup of coffee she makes me."

"No, she refused to tell me much." He retrieved a small yellow flower from the package of twelve and placed it into the ground.

Stella leaned over him and eyed the hole he'd dug. "Best not let Felecia see that."

"What?"

"The way you're planting that. You need to dig another couple inches or the roots won't be covered."

He removed the delicate flower and dug some more. "Why didn't you tell me?"

"Because it was more fun to correct you than instruct you on how to plant."

"Not about the flower. I knew the shop wasn't doing so well, but I didn't know the situation was so dire."

She stopped and raised a brow at him. "I thought you were smart. Have you seen one customer besides Bradley since you've been to my garage? No customers, no money. No money, no way to pay the rent."

"I'm sorry. If I'd known—"

"You would've what? I'm not taking charity. I told you that on day one," Stella huffed.

"Only Bradley's."

"That wasn't charity. It was a job." She pounded the dirt down around the roots of the flower she'd planted. "Now I'm not sure I even have that."

"What do you mean? I thought you were doing that car he brought here."

"That rare Porsche 916 I would have loved to restore, but without money I can't buy parts."

"Tell him you need the money."

"I did. He was supposed to send it by this morning, but it didn't appear in my bank account. He might have changed his mind after your outburst last night."

"I'm sorry. I know I overreacted. I should've trusted you to handle the situation yourself."

"Yes, you should have." She dropped the shovel. "Now that you know the truth, you can leave. No need to pretend you want to help any longer."

"I'm not pretending." He sat back on his heels and glanced around at the townspeople all working together. "I've never seen such a turnout of volunteers to help a neighbor. It doesn't seem possible. Drew kept telling me how special Sugar Maple is, but I didn't listen. Now I can see it for myself."

She looked up at him with a smile brighter than the sunlight reflecting off her shovel. "Are you trying to convince me to agree to your show?"

"No."

"Then the show is off?"

"No." He rested his hands in his lap, dirt tumbling down and over his knees. "I mean that I'd still love to do the show if you'd like to do it with me. I'll even advance you the money so that you can pay your rent."

Stella shook her head. "I wasn't being paid."

"Not directly, but since you'll have more business than you dreamed of once it airs, I know you're good for it."

"No, I'm not." She let out a long breath and shifted onto her other hip. "I'm not going to try to save the garage. It's too late. I'm not cut out to be a mechanic on these fancy machines the car companies are producing now."

"Then what will you do?" he asked.

"Don't know. I'll figure something out, though. I'm tough."

He put a hand on her forearm. "Yes, you are."

She slid her arm away. "We better get back to work."

"Stella?"

"Yes?"

"I do want to help you—not because you need the help,

since we all know how strong you are, but because I think you're an amazing woman who deserves more than she's been given in life."

She cringed away from him, and that's when he saw the truth behind Lori's words. If he wanted to connect with Stella, he needed to put them on an even playing ground. Could he tell her his deepest, darkest, most disastrous part of his life? Was he that strong?

He gripped the handle of the shovel and said a silent prayer for strength. "Stella, I want to tell you something. Something that might show you that you can trust me...or make you run from me. Either way, you'll know the truth. My truth."

She paused, as if waiting for him to tell her more, but he couldn't. Not only because he didn't want to relive his past, but there were too many people around to witness his meltdown.

"Not here. Can you meet me this evening? I'll bring burritos to your garage and we can talk then."

People moved around them, bustling with activity, but he and Stella sat still in the flowerbed for several moments.

"I promise not to try to save you from someone or feed you meat." He offered a half smile, and she reciprocated the gesture.

"Fine. Tonight. At seven." Stella returned to her work, so he followed her lead.

They worked all afternoon into early evening. Stella was right about one thing... The mysterious Jake inside had retrieved his coffee at some point when no one was looking.

The man remained behind the shield of his walls, crippled by his fear. It was time for Knox to let his fear go and live again. It was simple, yet terrifying. He stood on the porch, sweeping away the clippings and listening to the town courthouse bell ring. Each gong was like a punctuation on his past misery. At that moment, he realized the idea of sharing that part of him was too much to ask. He couldn't do it. Not even for Stella.

TWENTY-THREE

The crowd dispersed by the time the sun began to fade in the sky, but Knox continued to sweep the front porch. Stella had to give him credit... The man worked hard for a showbiz guy. He'd seemed less Internet personality and more wounded soldier all day. Perhaps it was the sun that had exhausted him. It had been a warmer day than normal. Spring weather was always unpredictable. One day hot, calling for shorts and T-shirt; the next day people had to wear sweaters or coats.

"Time to call it quits," Stella called up to him.

A bumblebee fluttered around her and then took off for open air. The new flowers drew all sorts of spring creatures into the landscape. Hummingbirds were her favorite, but they hadn't made an appearance today.

Knox rested his broom against the porch steps and joined her in the garden. "I'll see you in a couple of hours, right?"

If she were the romantic type, she'd notice the blooming flowers around them, the fading sun behind the trees casting a soothing glow over them, and the sound of crickets. But she wasn't the romantic type. "If you show, I'll see you," Stella said with more agitation than she'd intended.

"I'll be there." Knox strutted down the driveway and out of sight.

Stella gathered any remaining tools and put them in the wheelbarrow for Felicia to pick up.

"Whatcha doing out there?" Jake called from inside the doorway.

Stella froze. Her guilt had kept her moving until the last plant was in the ground in hopes Jake would come out to speak to them. Now that he'd appeared, she didn't know what to say. "Cleaning up."

The door creaked again. "Did you do all this?"

Stella shook her head. "No. The town did."

"Looked like Knox Brevard was here, too." Jake's head appeared between the gaping crack in the door. "You know, I've seen every one of his shows."

"Why?" Stella asked.

"Someone like me has a ton of time to watch shows and Internet series. I really liked the one he did that exposed that crooked home health organization."

"Sounds like a waste of time." She hiked up the stairs and leaned against the railing.

The door squeaked closed.

"You don't have to run. I'm not going to hurt you," Stella sighed.

The door reopened enough for her to see one of Jake's eyes. "I didn't want to do it, you know. But with Mama gone and me unable to work, the only income I have is rental properties around town. Trust me, the last person I want to kick out is you."

"Yeah, I understand. I don't blame you for hating me. I know I can be a little...abrasive."

"You mean downright frightening." Jake chuckled. "But that's part of why I've admired you since the fifth grade, when you stood up to the bully on the bus who threatened to pants me in front of the entire school."

"Pants you?" Stella tried to recall the memory, but it couldn't have been that important if she didn't remember it.

"You know, pull down my pants in front of everyone?" Jake said in an I've-got-a-secret voice Stella could barely hear, as if the underwear police were going to arrest him for wearing superman Underoos.

"That's terrible."

"Right, but you didn't let him." Jake sounded sweet and vulnerable. "I'm not scared of everything. It's just that I'm ill, and as much as I want to go see people in town, I equally don't want to step out of my home. Maybe I should've been brave enough to tell the collectors they could deal with me not paying the bills."

"I don't think that's the answer." Stella shifted, causing the banister to creak. She'd be back tomorrow to fix that.

"I just don't want to hurt you. You've been through enough in your life." Jake opened the door enough to see his nose and most of his mouth.

"We all have baggage. Listen, I have an idea. Instead of trying to race out of your home and see everyone, why don't you wait until I leave and then step out onto the front porch and look at your new garden?"

"Is it true that you called a Fabulous Five Intervention for me?"

"Don't know what you're talking about. Come out and see it or don't. But if you don't, you'll be missing something. Trust me. It'll be worth the few steps out to the porch, even if for only minutes. After that, maybe you'll be able to sit on the front porch and invite me over for coffee. You don't have to leave your home; just step onto your porch. Take it one step at a time. Tonight, flowers. Can you do that?"

"Don't know."

There was silence for almost a minute between them, and Stella wanted to stomp her foot and order him out to see the landscape. To see how much the town cared about him.

"I'll try. Not only for you, but for me."

"Good."

"Stella? Do you think you could come back tomorrow and ask me if I did it?"

"If you think that would help."

"I do." Jake remained in his spot, not wavering one direction or the other.

Her heart warmed at the thought of the people around Jake's home, showing their support, and it felt good. Too good. How could she be the one to cause him to lose the one thing he had in the world? She knew what it was like to cling to something from the past, only to feel it slip away. If she couldn't pay him, she had to tell him to sell. "Thank you."

"For what?"

She swallowed the dry lump of the past and thought about her own future. "For showing me that I will survive if I lose my grandfather's shop."

"You would give up your garage for me?"

She shrugged. "I can't make you wait any longer. I've been taking advantage of you for too long. You're a saint for putting up with me and my sparse payments over the last few years. You have a buyer for the land where my garage sits. You should take the offer." She pushed her sleeves up.

"If you do the show, you can make enough and you can pay me. That's what Ms. Horton said."

Stella rubbed her scalp and then dropped her hands to her legs with a loud thwap and headed down the front steps. "*If* I do the show." She paused at the edge of the sidewalk near the flowerbeds. "I mean, I know the town is counting on me, but I don't want to do it."

"Why not?" Jake asked.

"Because it isn't for me. My parents were the fame-seekers, not me." She swiped some remaining dirt from the sidewalk, studying the white flecks in the soil.

"Ha. You sure that's the only reason?"

"What else could it be?" Stella asked.

"Stella and Knox, sitting in a tree. K-I-S-S-I-N-G." Jake's voice sounded loud and clear, as if he wasn't cowering behind the door.

She looked up to see him standing at the railing. "Jake! You're, um—"

"Outside. Glad you can still think, despite having your brain mushed up by Knox. I never thought I'd see Stella turned around by a man. Love looks good on you."

Love? No. She wasn't capable of loving anyone. "What do you think?" She pointed at all the plants and trees. "Do you like it?"

"Nice avoidance." He scanned the front lawn, and tears filled his eyes.

"I didn't mean to upset you." Stella moved toward the porch. She wanted to comfort him, although she wasn't sure how. The girls always said that she'd run from a crying friend, or sit with a rigid posture and tap the person on the shoulder. Emotions were...uncomfortable.

"You didn't. These are tears of joy. I know Mama is looking down from heaven and smiling on you, Stella. Thank you." He fidgeted, shifting between his feet. Sweat dripped from his hairline.

"I'd like to thank the town." His voice came winded, words rushed. "I'd like to do it myself, but I'm not ready for that."

"You don't have to be scared. I'm here." Stella moved toward the porch once more.

Jake retreated a step. "I don't know if I can. But I also can't take your garage away. I'm not selling."

"You can't do that. You need the money."

"I can and I will. So you better find the money so we can both stay." Jake disappeared from her vantage point in the garden.

Her phone buzzed, and she looked at it to discover the money deposited into her account. It was her way out, but she didn't want a way out. She wanted to be brave like Jake.

"Tell you what," she said to Jake. "I'll do Knox's show, despite my fear, which might make me enough to pay you for a year, if you let me stay until the show airs and also get out there more yourself, despite whatever fear is holding you back."

He darted back inside the house. "Fine. You do Knox's show, and I'll start taking my meds and coming outside again. If only a few steps in the beginning." The door squealed. "Thank you, Stella. You're a good person, even if you don't believe that."

The door shut again. How could she let Jake down? The man had enough courage to come outside, despite his agoraphobia. Certainly she could face being on camera and dealing with the fame it could bring.

"I'll make this right, Jake. I promise that you won't lose your mama's home. And I won't lose my *abuelo's* garage."

Tonight she needed to dig deep into Knox's past, his idea for her future, and confront him. It was Knox's turn to deliver on his promise.

TWENTY-FOUR

Knox stood outside the garage with meatless burritos and a knot of apprehension in his gut. He tried to move, to knock, but his body froze. Froze from the realization that he had to open the door to something he'd closed a long time ago.

His pulse drummed in his ears. His heart hammered against his chest. Flashes of Alima's eyes, her tender touch, her belief that he would keep her safe in a war-torn country.

"Come in already. I'm hungry," Stella called from the three steps leading to a place he wanted to go but was struggling with the path to get there. She'd worn the white dress. Somehow she'd removed the stains, and in the glowing yellow porch light, she looked like a dark-haired angel.

"I can't. I thought I could. But I can't. I'm sorry." He about-faced but then remembered the burritos. Before he could think, he marched to her and held out the bag. "Here, I'm sorry. I...I can't."

"Then we'll eat." She retrieved the bag and then took his hand. "You're shaking. Come inside."

He hated himself for being weak. There was nothing worse

than showing someone you were damaged goods, not worthy of real affection. "I'm not the man you think I am."

Stella didn't even blink. "I think you're more than you give yourself credit for."

He followed her inside, despite his stomach and chest burning with warning. The 916's hood was open, and tools were around it. Irritation erupted, covering his fear. "You're working on his car?"

"Yes," Stella said in a matter-of-fact tone.

"I see." He pulled his captive hand from her and moved away to think, kicking a wrench that clanked across the floor.

"He already paid me." Stella touched his back.

"I guess it's for the best. You might not believe this, but I want you to save your garage." He turned and found himself in her arms, a circle of warmth and comfort he didn't deserve, so he broke free and paced the gray, oil-stained floor until he discovered a blanket with candles. A bottle of wine rested on ice. A scene of seduction he wanted to star in without any backstory. Stella had believed they could move forward into a new kind of relationship, one he wanted more than the air in the room, but he couldn't. He didn't deserve love. He didn't deserve Stella.

"I have the money to pay Jake. This is a win for everyone." Stella knelt on the blanket, poured wine into a glass, and held it out for him. He wanted to leave, but he couldn't bring himself to go.

He took the glass and unceremoniously downed two gulps. The citrus flavor lingered for a second and then faded from his tongue. "I'm telling Lori that I won't move forward with the streaming project and we'll do the segment on the clothing store."

"What about your dream for television?" Stella lingered near him but didn't make a move to touch him again.

"It doesn't matter. It wasn't meant to be." He could feel

Stella so close and yet so far away. "I've concentrated on this dream career for the last decade. It was fun and I don't regret it, but I want more in my life."

"Like what?" Stella nudged the burrito bag out of the way and tapped the blanket. The rough edges of her personality had been sanded away, and all he could see was her sweet, caring side."

"I want a life like yours," he blurted before his mind ever processed the idea.

"Mine?" She scanned the room.

He didn't know if it was the wine or her, but his heartbeat slowed and he wanted to stay a little longer. He knelt by her and set the wineglass on the ground behind him. "Yes. Don't you see how amazing your life is here in Sugar Maple? You may not have riches or fame, but you have something better. You have a town-family. One who would do anything for you and who you would do anything for. I didn't get it when I first arrived. I thought you were all backwards and crazy. But when I was working the garden today, I saw it. The unconditional love that only comes from family. I didn't understand before today. But the "neighbors looking out for neighbors" mentality is almost like brothers of war. An inexplicable bond that forms through intense situations."

"You're right. I do have a modest but good life here. That's probably why I've lived this poor for so long."

"I just don't want to see you suffer. I want to protect and care for you." Nervous energy catapulted him into action. He shoved from the ground, his breaths short and fast.

"Why?"

He paced and fought the stinging, nerve-gnawing pain eating away at his insides. "Because I couldn't save Alima." He grabbed his head, the flashes like a strobe light sending sharp pain through his skull behind his eyes.

A hand rubbed small circles on his back. Another hand held tight to his bicep. "You lost someone in Iraq, and it haunts you still today," she said in a hesitant tone, but with a hint of confidence.

The muscles in his arms shook, tears stung his eyes, but he could feel her tiny hands slide halfway around him and her cheek rest to his chest.

Comfort.

It frightened him, and he wanted to shove her away and run far from here, far from the memories, but he resisted, closing his eyes tight to stay in control.

They stood there for several minutes until his breath slowed, his heart didn't thrash against his chest. "I'm sorry. Excuse me." He tried to slide away, but she didn't let him go. She held tight as if she'd never let him fall into his pit of grief again.

"You've carried a secret that has corroded you from the inside out." She hugged him tight to her and then released him enough to look up at him.

He didn't want to see the pity in her eyes, but when he looked down, he was surprised. All he saw was compassion and understanding.

"You'll never heal if you keep pushing people away. Trust me, I know." She stood strong before him, but how long would her strength keep her safe? "I won't force you to tell me, but I won't lie. I'm disappointed. I thought there was something happening here." She slipped away, like the scarf from Alima's head.

He grabbed the back of the lawn chair sitting near the 916 and bent the frame. "There is."

"Then talk to me. We both know that you have a choice to make here and now. You've tortured yourself long enough. And if I'm being honest, I hope whatever this is between us moves forward. I'd hate for this to end before it ever begins. But I won't be another girl on your arm to show off until you get too close. We're either real, or we don't happen."

"She died because she loved me and she trusted the wrong person." He spit the words out, but the bitterness remained.

The clock on the wall ticked slower than his pulse. He thought he'd fall to his knees and scream at God, but he didn't. The three-thousand-pound missile piercing his heart flaked and fell from him. Shrapnel remained with sharp edges, but that could be removed piece by piece.

Stella lifted her chin and then walked over to the blanket and sat down. "I know how hard that was for you to say. For now, why don't you sit by my side and we can relax? The Band-Aid's been ripped off, but your wound's raw. I can wait until you want to tell me more."

"No. I can't believe I'm going to say this, but I want to tell you." Knox slumped. "You need to know what kind of man I am before you decide to let anything between us move forward."

"You're a brave and caring person who has been through a lot," Stella said in a soft voice.

"I don't know about that."

"We're the same. Wounded, untrusting, and lonely because we've kept everyone at a distance to protect ourselves from more pain." Stella patted the blanket next to her. "You can trust me. Heck, I put on a dress for you."

"No heels, though." He pointed to her bare feet.

"They turned back into some inanimate object, and if I don't eat soon, I'll turn into a pumpkin," she said with a grin.

"I don't think your slippers were glass, and you don't strike me as the fairy godmother–wishing type," Knox teased.

"I think Ms. Horton could play the fairy godmother part well." Stella half shrugged.

Knox noticed that he wasn't gripping the chair as if it were his lifeline and his breath and pulse had calmed. Stella had done that. He wanted to tell her everything and pray she would still want to be with him. "You know you're special. You're strong and independent, yet you have a softer side."

"Don't go telling people that. I like being unapproachable. Besides, I'm not good with the girly gossip and crying-over-a-man stuff. We don't want to give the girls the wrong impression. Lord knows I taught Jackie to never braid my hair after the kindergarten finger-painting incident."

He returned to Stella's side, this time settling in, relaxing, and putting his legs out in front of him. It was time. They were alone. No one else could hear his failures. No one could post them on the Internet for the world to read about. He'd spent so much time running from his past. He was exhausted and wanted to rest. Perhaps now he would be able to sleep. "I didn't mean to fall in love, but I was young and naïve. Perhaps I was even a little bit of a romantic."

Stella didn't say anything, but her lip twitched into a knowing grin. That's when he realized she'd already seen that in him, considering the candles and the wine. She hadn't staged that for herself. She'd done that for him, dress and all. She deserved to know the entire truth. "Alima—" saying her name aloud caused him to take in a stuttered breath "—was a local woman in an Iraqi village we were occupying in order to protect the villagers."

Stella took his hand and held it tight, letting him know she was there and he was safe.

"I thought Alima was strong and smart and loved me, but in the end I was wrong. So wrong." He closed his eyes, and images slid into view. "I should've seen the signs. She'd bring me food and sneak away from her family to speak with me. I was careful since the prejudice against the occupying American soldiers had reached epic proportions after an incident involving an entire family in a nearby village. It was war, but going in I thought we were the good guys." He snorted. "A young man's view."

She didn't say anything. She only sat in silence with an attentive tilt to her head and gaze zeroed in on him.

"Our relationship changed from acquaintances to friends to falling in love. We were there long enough to set up a routine, and despite the men ready to move on to the next battle, I was content with remaining. But the war caught up, and it was headed our way. I knew the villagers would be executed or worse, so I made arrangements to get Alima to a safer area. I vowed to return and marry her the minute I had leave, and then I'd work on moving her to the States. I thought I was giving her the world. I never thought she wouldn't want to leave the war-torn home she had always known."

He stopped for a moment, eyeing the dark hole of loss. He'd blocked the memories for so long, it unnerved him to face them again. Perhaps he'd said enough for one day.

Stella rubbed her thumb over his hand, caressing and massaging the fear from him.

"One day I was supposed to meet with her family for coffee. An honor that appeared to seal our plans. I knew this invitation meant their approval of our plan and ultimately our marriage, but I was wrong." He sucked in a deep, oil and gasoline–scented breath. "I was delayed by my commanding officer, and when I arrived..." He swallowed the lump of regrets. "When I arrived and saw Alima in the doorway, the home exploded."

Stella squeezed his fingers. "I'm so sorry."

"It gets worse. She'd set it up. She'd sacrificed herself, me... us in exchange for her family."

Stella rose to her knees and cradled his head to her chest.

His arms, legs, shoulders shook. Her heartbeat soothed him enough to keep him from screaming. "Every night, when I close my eyes, I see the headscarf I gave her float away in the air, the way it did the day of the explosion. Why did she trust those savages over me?"

"I don't think she did. She chose her family over her own life, and you were collateral damage. I wasn't there, but according to the news, that's how the extremist groups work. They manipulate by focusing on loyalty and terror."

"No, she set me up."

"Did she?"

He pulled away, blinking through his tear-filled eyes. "Didn't you hear what I said?"

"Yes, but did you ever think about the fact that you weren't inside the building when it blew?"

"That's because I was late."

Stella caressed his cheek. "I think she sacrificed herself to save all of you. If the bomb went off early, I think she did that. Can you remember how the bomb exploded?"

The world stopped rotating around him. His entire existence paused, and he rewound to that day. "I can see the door open. She steps out wearing the headscarf and...a...vest." The air rushed into his lungs, the world spun out of control... He pressed his hand to the ground at his side to keep him from falling over. "Suicide?"

TWENTY-FIVE

For the first time in years, a man had stolen Stella's attention, despite her best effort to keep distance between them. When Knox had shown up at Jake's place and dug in the dirt at her side, she'd realized Knox Brevard was more than just an Internet personality. There were more layers to him. There was something special about Knox. Now she saw him as a compassionate, caring, charismatic man with a wounded heart.

After several clicks of the clock's second hand, she let out a breath she'd held in for as long as she could. "You know it's not your fault that Alima made that choice. If you're honest with yourself, you'll see that all you did was try to save her from a horrible situation."

"I can hear those words, but it doesn't mean that I can accept them. I'm tired of holding on to the guilt for so many years, though. I guess I thought I didn't deserve a life if she didn't have one, too. And I thought I could never trust another person after she'd betrayed me like that."

"I'm realizing that trust is something we all struggle with in one form or another."

He scooted closer, knee-to-knee, eye-to-eye, soul-to-soul.

"I've never trusted anyone enough to tell them about Alima, not even Drew. I hope you know how much it means that I could trust you"

Stella felt the sting of tears and blinked them away, knowing that if he had trusted her with his deepest secret, she could finally trust him having hers. "Knowing that helps. I guess we'll both have to work on our trust issues, but...I'm glad I can trust you, too."

The aroma of the burritos made her stomach growl, reminding her she hadn't eaten all day. "Sorry," she said, feeling her face warm with embarrassment

"Please, eat." His thumb brushed over her knuckle, distracting her from hunger to more primal needs.

"No, I'll wait."

He swallowed hard enough for her to hear. "I think we've both been waiting a long time. I don't know about you, but I'm tired of waiting."

His fingers grazed her chin, caressed her cheek, brushed her ear. The closeness, the feeling of his fingers sweeping over her skin stoked an excitement inside her and a calmness she hadn't felt in years. This man in front of her wasn't like other men she'd known. As Ms. Horton would say, he was true of heart.

"I am, too." She lunged into him and captured his lips.

He rose onto his knees wrapping his strong arms around her and pulling her close. His mouth was like spring: fresh, welcoming, and invigorating. She lost herself in the kiss that stole memories of all other kisses. Her body swelled with hope, and her insides turned to mush. She melted into him, surrendering to his affections and praying they could find a little happiness together.

Everything blurred until his passion changed to soft, sweeping kisses down her face and neck. When he sat back, she collapsed onto her hip, and they both sat with wide eyes, panting.

Their chests rose and fell at the same rapid cadence. The clock on the wall ticking away came into focus. A car passed on the street.

Knox entwined his fingers with hers. "I have an idea. I thought it might be too crazy, but now I believe anything's possible." He took a deep breath, as if to replenish what he'd lost a few moments earlier. "Hear me out, okay?"

She nodded, scared she'd sound like Mary-Beth discovering a jewelry sale, high-pitched and way too excited.

"You've been trying so hard to keep your grandfather's garage open and the same as when he ran it, but life isn't the same now."

She looked to the ground, feeling her failures too powerful to face, but he tipped her chin up to face him.

"It isn't your fault. The car industry has gone through a computer revolution, but you still love the old world of getting your hands dirty. I respect that. It's one of the things I like about you. You're true to yourself, and I can't bear to see you change. You're perfect the way you are. That's why I think that if you agree to do the show, we should focus on the restoration, not on the fixing cars side of things."

Her gaze snapped to his. "But—"

"I'm going to have Drew run an analysis, but it doesn't take a public relations and business analysis to know there's an opportunity with your skill set. I did a quick search and found places that charge a fortune to have this done. I believe we should run my segment on your 1957 Chevy—or the 916 if you prefer—and show you working on the restoration. I believe it'll generate a ton of business for you and it'll be what you need to get out of debt and live a better life. And the only thing I'm offering is my platform, no strings attached. I only offer you an opportunity. Because Stella Frayser, you don't need anyone to take care of you." He squeezed her fingers. "That doesn't mean you don't need anyone in your life, though."

His hands trembled, and she realized how much he'd put himself out there for her. A man who'd been closed off for so long, and he trusted her. Not only with his secrets but with his affections.

"What do you think?" His voice sounded low, searching.

"I think you're brilliant." Stella scanned the garage, realizing she'd been chasing the wrong path. "My *abuelo* would love this idea."

"Great. I know you don't love the camera, but I need to run a promo to start advertising, and then we'll get the filming started next week." He released her fingers and held out his hand. "Deal?"

"Deal." She shook but then pulled him close for another kiss.

TWENTY-SIX

A fluttering in Knox's chest made him want to keep moving, but he needed to focus. This promo had to wow his fans into watching the next segment. He hadn't been this excited since he'd started his show years ago. "Thanks for agreeing to do this last minute, and Drew, thanks for the marketing research. I know you've already secured another job, so I thank you for your time."

"Who are you, and what have you done with my best friend?" Drew set the camera tripod up and then the two main lights.

Knox glanced up to the loft to see if Mary-Beth and the other girls were done making Stella camera ready. He could see her smacking their hands away from her face and refusing to wear jewelry. Good for her.

Lori set out the microphone and closed the curtain behind the sink. "You're doing the right thing here."

"It's a shame that our team will be breaking up. I forgot how well we all worked together. I guess that's why our show went viral from the third episode." Knox thought back over the years and all they'd accomplished together, yet Drew looked happier now than he ever had, thanks to Carissa, and Lori even seemed less stressed while living in Sugar Maple. Knox knew her well enough to see she didn't want to leave this small town. And if he was being honest with himself, neither did he.

"We don't have to break up the gang," Drew said, drawing both Lori's and Knox's attention.

Lori leaned against the table where all the equipment was set up. "What do you mean?"

Drew typed something on his laptop and turned it around. "I think we could run a new program from here. Knox 2.0, if you will. The numbers are higher than ever since we ran the bakery and a few promo segments of the town. Perhaps it's the state the world is in right now, but your fans care less about who is on your arm and more about escaping to Sugar Maple. Look at all those comments. Not one of them is about who Knox is dating this week. They all want to know about when the mayor is getting married and how the girl in Sugar Maple makes the perfect cup of coffee."

"How do they even know all that?" Knox asked.

Drew clicked a button, and a Sugar Maple website popped up with a news tab that showed videos and copy about the town. The most recent entry, entitled "Wedding Update" with a picture of the girls trying on dresses, had over a thousand comments. "You can thank Lori for doing all the work."

"And Drew for putting it together. People are eating this up." Lori pointed at the screen. "It ties in with your show, but there's extra behind-the-scenes and details added."

"So more about the town than about me." Knox scanned the page.

"For now, but we have a plan to tie it all together."

He realized they thought he cared. "I think this is perfect. I'm getting tired of traveling all over the world, and I don't need to anymore. I'm not trying to run from or to anything. I was thinking I wanted to extend the show here so that I could stay longer and find what you both have in this little town."

Lori patted his back. "Oh, honey. I think you've already found it."

Stella cleared her throat, and they all turned to find her at the bottom of the stairs. And she looked perfect. She wore her overalls, but her hair was shiny and bouncy, makeup accentuated her dark eyes, and her lips were full and kissable.

"Too much?" Stella asked. "I told Mary-Beth I was done with all the fussing."

"She wouldn't even let me put on these darling car earrings. Look, they're little Chevys."

"I agree. No earrings." Knox walked across the garage and took Stella by the hands. "You look perfect the way you are." He leaned in. "Don't get me wrong, I love the white dress, too. But nothing is better than you in your element."

Redness crept down Stella's cheeks and disappeared beneath the white T-shirt she wore under the overalls.

"Oh my goodness, did you just make our Stella blush?" Mary-Beth said loud enough that her voice echoed in the shop.

Carissa and Felicia raced down the stairs to Stella. "No way."

Stella elbowed Mary-Beth and glowered at the other two.

Jackie stood at the balcony of the loft looking down over them as if an outsider. He wanted to make her happy, but not at Stella's expense. He'd go by and see Jackie later to try to smooth things over and tell her that they'd run some promo for her shop next week.

"You ready?" He tugged her toward the set. "Be yourself and don't worry about the camera."

"Am I supposed to look at it and speak toward it?"

"Just look at me if you're not looking at the engine." Knox took her by the hand and led her to the car. She held tight to him, and he loved it. The realization that this beautiful, dedicated, loyal woman wanted to be around him made him feel more important than any time he'd won an award or been recognized for his show. This wasn't make-believe, this was real, and he wanted to embrace it. "You work on something under the hood, and then after my intro, I'll have you answer a question... and then we'll be done. It's only a teaser for the episode."

"I can do that. I'm happy to hide behind the hood." She darted out of the field of view of the camera, so he had to nudge her back into view. "No hiding. You still need to be working in the background."

She did a full-body shake, as if she were about to enter a fighting ring. "Okay, I'm ready."

"Quiet, everyone," Drew ordered.

Knox checked Stella's placement one more time and then stepped forward. "Hello. I'm Knox Brevard, and I'm excited to share our next segment with you, airing in only a few weeks." He held his head high and stepped toward the camera. "First, I want to thank all of you viewers for your support. It's obvious that you've fallen in love with the town of Sugar Maple, based on your comments posted all over social media, the website, and here on my channel." He smiled and stepped back from the camera. "Based on your outcry for more, we are pleased to announce our next segment with the amazing and talented Stella Frayser, who owns and operates her own car restoration company." A wrench dropped behind him, and the room fell silent.

"Sorry, you surprised me. I didn't mean to interrupt you and ruin it." She retrieved the wrench and shot up to her full height.

Knox saw how tense and freaked out she looked, and he didn't like it. He stole a moment with her behind the hood. "No need. We can edit around this. You didn't ruin anything." He toyed with her soft hair around her face. "You've got nothing to worry about. We can film this fifty times if we need to. There isn't any pressure at all. Got it?"

Her shoulders dropped and she nodded. "Okay. I got it. Relax."

"Hey, look at me. You said you trusted me, right?" He drew her close, capturing her gaze with his. "I won't let you look any less perfect than the woman you are."

"Then this will be a disaster," Stella joked.

Jackie rounded the car and tapped her toes at them. "Hate to break up your little meeting, but we have plans to help Ms. Horton with picking out flowers before she and Mr. Strickland leave town tomorrow to go visit his son. And Lori has to fly back to LA for some meetings tonight."

He wasn't sure why Jackie had stuck around. Stella had told him they'd all be here in support of her. It was the Fabulous Five's way. He guessed it was more out of jealousy that Jackie came around and hoped Stella would watch her back.

Stella nudged away from him and snagged the wrench. "I'm ready."

He returned to face Drew behind the camera, Lori at Drew's side. He gave them a nod and then found the spot where he'd been standing. "I've visited many car repair shops and restoration locations during my years as a host of this show. I'm sure you all remember the last one." He shook his head, knowing that if he didn't mention it, the comments would blow up about him ignoring the obvious failure from his past. This way he could get ahead of it. "This shop is run by the most talented person I've ever met. She doesn't only restore cars... She does it with authenticity and a love for each vehicle. Let's take a look at the car she's working on now."

Stella looked up with a smile, and he knew she'd already won the audience over before she even spoke.

"Stella, can you tell us what kind of vehicle this is and why it's special to you?"

"Yes, of course. This is a 1957 Chevrolet Bel Air. This car has belonged to my family since before I was born. It was a car that I worked on with my *abuelo,* who started this garage. He's the one who instilled the love and respect I have for fine classic cars."

Knox was so caught up watching her face animate with passion and the way she spoke that he forgot he was running the promo. "Right. Um..." He paused to gather himself. "We are so glad you agreed to do this show with us. I don't know about you, but I'm excited to get started. Thank you so much for inviting us into your garage and behind the scenes." He turned toward the camera. "The story of Sugar Maple doesn't end there. As a special thank-you, we'll be showing you even more about this special town over the next several months. Starting next week, we'll be interviewing residents so that they can answer your questions directly. But don't miss our next segment with this special woman, who will capture your attention and heart the way she has mine." He scooped her into his arms and kissed her in front of Drew, Lori, the rest of the Fabulous Five, and all his viewers.

TWENTY-SEVEN

The morning sun rising high into a cloudless sky promised the best spring day. Stella reached Maple Grounds and found it to be standing-room only. To her relief, she spotted Carissa, Felicia, and Jackie at the corner bistro table. Hopefully she could convince them all to leave and give her the table when Knox arrived.

"Hi, ladies." Stella sat in the empty chair.

"What fairy princess visited you last night with cheerful pixie dust?" Jackie said with a nose scrunch.

Stella eyed the place and wished there was outdoor seating. "No one. Can't a girl enjoy spring without an inquisition?"

Carissa smiled. "That's nice. Are you meeting up with Knox this morning?"

"Yes, in about twenty minutes." Stella tucked her hair behind her ear. She wasn't used to wearing it down during the day.

"That's nice. You can have our table when he comes and we'll skedaddle." Felicia touched Stella's shoulder, and it didn't even bother her. Progress.

IF YOU ADORE ME   159

IF YOU ADORE ME   159

"Haven't you seen enough of him?" Jackie rolled her eyes and took a sip of her coffee.

The crowd rumbled behind them, so Stella was grateful to be in the corner. "Considering someone kept us so late last night that I stood Knox up for dinner... Coffee is a nice peace offering."

"Nice? You?" Jackie rested her elbows on the table and leaned in. "Who are you, and what did you do with our friend Stella?"

"Cute." She eyed the counter, jonesing for a caffeine fix, but that line looked daunting.

Carissa stood. "I'll get your drink. Mary-Beth said she'd make one when she saw you walk in. I'm sure it's behind the counter."

Felicia snuggled in closer to her. "Do you realize what Knox did last night? It's so romantic. I wish I knew a man who was so caught up with me that he didn't care about the rest of the world."

"What are you talking about?" Stella asked.

"I'm talking about the fact that Knox Brevard declared his love for you by kissing you during the promo. He told the world he was taken and no other woman could compare to you." Felicia squealed and clapped her hands together.

"Puh-leeeease. You got all that from one kiss?" Jackie's cheeks tightened.

An excitement tingled inside her, and it frightened her. No need to get ahead of anything. "Jackie has a point. You're reading way too much into this."

"Did you just agree with me?" Jackie pressed a palm to her forehead in a faux swoon. "Dear Lord, I think the world is ending."

Carissa plopped a cup of coffee in front of Stella. "Unfortunately, Mary-Beth was so slammed she didn't even see you come in, so this is what you get for now."

"What's going on? Why's it so busy?" Stella asked.

Carissa pointed outside the window to a big bus. "It's that tour company. They're stopping in town. I had to prepackage sixty bakery items by seven this morning. Drew says I need to hire someone before he quits."

"Good idea. Maybe you could put up a flyer or something," Felicia offered.

"I'll try, but I dislike hiring staff." Carissa sighed.

"No, you hate *firing* staff. You're too nice." Stella eyed the coffee but didn't partake. "Tell you what... I'll take care of firing for you if you hire someone."

"Now that's the Stella we know." Jackie lifted her coffee in a toast, downed the last bit, and then stood. "Looks like it's time for us to go. Lover boy's here."

The way Jackie said lover boy made him sound like a married man sneaking out on his wife. Apparently Carissa caught her tone too, based on the fact she swished her lips and narrowed her gaze at Judas Jackie. Not that it would do any good.

Stella turned and waved, her pulse increasing at the sight of Knox. He pointed to the line to order and joined it, allowing her more time with her friends. That man was amazing, skilled in the art of women and their needs. Guess practice makes perfect, as Ms. Melba would say.

She returned her attention back to the girls, but a man walking by the window outside with tuffs of gray hair hanging from the edges of his hat caught her attention. She blinked several times, reconciling the image with her memories. "It can't be," she mumbled. A coldness settled into her bones.

"What?" Felicia asked.

The man disappeared from her sight. She went to the

window and peered out, but there was no sight of him in the town square. She shook her head. "Geesh, I think I need more sleep."

"You okay?" Carissa joined her with a worried, pinched-brow expression.

Stella cleared her throat. "Yes, everything's fine. My crazy head has been playing tricks on me since all this production stuff started."

"You mean since you fell in love," Felicia said and then skittered out the door before Stella could react. Smart girl.

The girls flooded out of the coffee shop, leaving Stella in the corner surrounded by patrons. She eyed the outside world and decided it would be a much better spot to be with Knox right now, so she gave up the table and joined him in line. "Hey, I'm sorry about last night. I wanted to go to dinner with you, but Ms. Horton won't return for a week. That meant I was guilted into staying late for girl time."

"No worries at all." He kissed her cheek, waking her up despite the lack of caffeine.

Stella eyed the crowd. "You want to abandon this mission and go for a walk?"

The line edged forward, and someone shouted an order up. His smile crept up higher than she'd ever seen it. "I'm afraid I was up all night thinking about this girl who keeps distracting me, so I need some caffeine. How about you go find a nice spot in the square for us to sit, and I'll bring you something there."

"Sounds perfect." She stood with him for another moment, holding on to his arm and leaning her head on his shoulder. "I confess I may have suffered the same ailment. I managed to start work on the 916 since I was up, though. A part of me is excited about doing the show. Of course, another part of me wants to run for the mountains."

His shoulder stiffened. "I hope you don't run. And not for the sake of the show but for me."

She lifted her head and saw the muscles in his cheeks and jaw strain. "Don't worry. I won't run."

He took her in his arms and kissed her head. "I'm glad to hear that."

"Good 'cause you're stuck with me for a while." Stella stood by his side a few moments, realizing what she'd said. They would be together working on the show, and for the first time, she was curious and excited to see what tomorrow could offer.

She stood on her toes and pressed a kiss to his cheek and then headed outside so she could snag the perfect seat under the bright maple tree in the center of the square.

She sat for several moments, watching birds swoop in and out of trees, enjoying the fresh mountain air with a hint of oak. Deep down, she hoped for Carissa's reality, or at least a version of it, but she couldn't comprehend a man who sought fame and fortune like her parents had ever being content with remaining in Sugar Maple.

No. She wouldn't self-sabotage this for no reason.

"Hello, sweet girl." Her father's gravelly voice shattered the tranquility of the spring day.

So much for not self-sabotaging. This had to be her inner voice scaring her away or something. There was no way her father could be here. Ms. Horton had made sure of that a long time ago. But the hair on the back of her neck was standing like porcupine quills.

She shot up from the bench to find the man who'd run off with her mother, only to return alone and torture her with his drunken fantasies and desperation, standing behind her. The man who once tortured her with his drinking and friends and ideas of how to get money to feed his addiction had dared to return to Sugar Maple. He stood there with a sharp grimace and small beady eyes. Prison hadn't been kind, leaving a scar down the side of his face and wrinkles with patches of discolored skin.

She was suddenly cold, despite the warm day. Her hands shook. Her mouth went dry. "You're supposed to be in jail."

"Out on good behavior." He smiled, revealing chipped teeth, but his dimples showed. The ones that always seemed to make women fall for his lies.

"Doesn't explain why you're here." She moved over so the bench remained between them.

"This is my home." He waved his arms like a king declaring his country. "Besides, where else would I go? I have a garage to run here in town."

She fisted her hands and thought she'd breathe fire. "There's nothing you own here in town. The garage is mine. You need to leave."

"I'm afraid, little girl, you're wrong. Your mother and I would be the beneficiaries of any of his property."

"You need to leave," Stella said in a hostile tone.

"No, you're wrong. Besides, I'm not going anywhere. You wouldn't send your only living relative that wants you away, would you? Not like your mother has any love for you. I'm all you got."

Stella eyed the square and knew he was wrong. She had a town-family. What she didn't want was her town-family knowing anything about what had happened all those years ago. "I have no family. You need to leave."

He rounded the bench and closed the distance between them. "Don't be like that, sweet girl. I'm home now. And we can be family again. Come on, I've changed. You wouldn't leave your father out in the cold, would you?"

This didn't feel like a father coming home. He felt like a nightmare coming to life.

TWENTY-EIGHT

"What's going on?" Knox could only see Stella's back as he approached, but she was tense. He'd spent enough time with her to recognize the signs of her being distressed.

She whirled around, showing him it was more than stress. That was fear in her wide eyes and open mouth.

He shot in front of her. "Who are you, and what do you want?"

The man's lips curled into a menacing grin. "Didn't know my daughter had to have a man to take care of her."

"Daughter?" He squeezed the paper cups in his hands so tight, the lids popped off and hot coffee exploded over his fingers. He tossed the cups to the ground and stepped forward, not even feeling the pain of the liquid burning him. "You're not welcome here. Leave."

The man laughed. "Who is this stranger that thinks he can tell a born and raised Sugar Maplean how to do something? Especially with my own flesh and blood. Oh wait, that's right... You're that prissy Internet guy. The one making videos about my sweet town."

Stella grabbed Knox's arm and pulled him to her side. "Don't feign any love for this town. Leave, or I'll call the sheriff."

"Go ahead. I'm not doing anything wrong. No reason to arrest me. I have a right to come home."

People crowded around and whispered to one another. Why weren't they running this man out of town before he could cause Stella any more harm, Knox wondered. Even if they didn't know the full extent of the damage he'd caused, certainly they could see the man was no good and needed to be sent away.

"It doesn't matter. Let's go." Stella yanked Knox away. She hotfooted it through the square and up the hill.

Knox wanted to call his war buddies and have them help take care of this so-called father. That was the kind of bond brothers had, but that's not how this sweet little town handled their business. He walked backwards, headed after Stella. "Stay away from her."

Knox raced up the hill after her, not wanting her out of his sight with the threat in town. She moved so fast, it took him to the edge of the gravel lot before he caught up to her. "Wait. Stella, talk to me. What can I do?"

"Nothing." She marched up the three steps to the door and swung it open. He barely got over the threshold before she slammed it shut and locked it and the deadbolt. "He's not getting in here. He said he was here to take the garage as his own. He doesn't deserve even a piece of my *abuelo's* legacy. My grandfather hated the man."

"Then I'll hire an attorney, and I'll make sure he doesn't take it," Knox vowed.

"No." Stella threw her hands up in the air. "You don't get it. My father doesn't play by the rules. If he wants this place, he'll find a way to get it or destroy it if he can't have it for himself."

"Then I'll hire security." He grabbed her hand to stop her

pacing so she'd listen to him, but she pulled away from him. He hated watching Stella in distress. The rock-solid woman who handled everything with grit and confidence looked lost and afraid. It churned his insides with burning acidic anger. His desire to take down the enemy overwhelmed him, but this wasn't war. This situation didn't have rules of engagement.

"You can't save me from this. I'm the only one who can handle my father. You need to go before you get caught in the crossfire."

He saw it, her desire to run and keep her troubles from anyone else. To lock up anything she didn't want to share. He wouldn't let her pull away like that, not when he'd just managed to crack the vault on her feelings. "I'm not leaving you. Not now, not with him in town." Knox wanted to scream, to shake her until she saw reason, but he knew her strategy. She wasn't trying to protect herself but him from her father.

"You have to. You'll only make things worse," she said in a soft tone. "When my father is cornered, he lashes out in a way people don't expect."

Knox took a moment, forced his anger down, and spoke in the calmest voice possible. "Then educate me, and we'll deal with this together. I won't stand by and let this man ruin your life. Alone you won't stand a chance. Together we are stronger."

Sweat trickled down his neck. The heat of the spring sun with the windows and doors closed and no air conditioning was causing the temperature in the room to rise, or was it his fear heating him?

"No. I'm weak when you're around me." Her cold tone sent an icy chill through him. "You think you know my father, but you don't. If you're here when he comes around, then he won't listen to any deal I can make with him. He wants money, not this garage. He must've seen or heard about the show and thinks I'm getting paid some outrageous sum, and he wants a piece of it. A large slice would be more accurate. That's what my father does. He uses people to get money to feed his addiction." She straightened, turned with a soft smile, and touched Knox's cheek with distracting affection. "You said you trust me. I'm asking you to show that you meant that."

"I do, but there's no way I'm leaving you alone with that man coming here."

"I won't be alone. I'll call the sheriff and let him know what's going on. He's an old friend with no love for my father, and that way if my father gets out of hand, he'll arrest him." She sounded certain of her plan, but Knox didn't like it.

"I thought you said if your father saw anyone else around, he wouldn't listen to any deal."

"He won't see the sheriff unless things go south." Stella pressed a kiss to his lips, blurring his vision of protection and concern. "Trust me. I know how to handle this situation. I can't believe I'm saying this, but I love that you want to protect me. I've never had that in my life."

"I know, and that tears me up inside. You deserve to have a protector who cares for you. It might be hard for you to accept, but I'm here. Let me help."

"No. You being here won't help."

"I'll offer him money to go. You need your funds to save your garage. I know you don't want me giving you money, but I'm not. I'm paying this man to...to leave so he won't ruin my show." Even he heard the lie in his words. This had nothing to do with his show.

"It won't work. If he thinks there is any way he can score some cash, he'll never leave. And if I give him any, it will never be enough. Please, let me handle this the right way and send my father back to jail, where he can't pop up every time there's a possibility of money."

Everything inside Knox screamed for him to stay by her

side, but he knew that she would hate him if he didn't give her space. That didn't mean he couldn't stay nearby and watch and be ready to help. He'd leave the garage, but he wouldn't leave her unprotected. "Fine. But I don't like this."

She kissed him. A passionate kiss. A kiss he recognized.

A goodbye kiss.

TWENTY-NINE

The garage hadn't felt so empty since Stella's *abuelo* had died. She was alone, which was what she wanted. Her father would dredge up and twist everything to make her look like a freak. Her friends wouldn't believe the lies, but they'd never look at her the same again. The shame filled her the way it had that day when she was rescued from that barn and ushered to her grandparents for good.

She sat in her lawn chair, facing the door and holding her wrench. The man had once been a father who protected her, loved her, cared for her, even if from a distance while pursuing his dreams. But once her mother left him, he'd changed. The sweet man turned into an angry drunk. The more he drank, the more his mind altered to a state where she couldn't even recognize the man anymore. Even when she'd seen him in the town square today, she'd noticed his pupils were wide, despite the bright sunshine.

All day, she waited for the man, but there wasn't a knock at the door. When the sun began to fade and the light dimmed inside the gray, oversized room, she began to doubt her decision to send Knox away.

No, she knew what she needed to do. Money. That's what he wanted. She'd finish the 916 and give him the money, but there was no way he'd get the garage. The one her *abuelo* swore her father would never be welcome in again.

Maybe she should've considered Knox's offer... No. It wasn't an option. The corruption scandal would ruin Knox's show forever. She had no doubt that her father would take to any media stream possible to share his relationship with Knox Brevard. She couldn't let that happen. Of course, once the money was gone and the garage sold, her father wouldn't have a reason to return.

She slipped her phone from her pocket and texted Jake.

How quick can you sell the property? I won't make the payments. Sorry.

Three dots danced on the screen until words popped up.

Immediately. But you have more time. I gave you thirty days.

She fought the tears pricking at her eyes and knew she'd made the right decision. And when her father arrived, it would be the quickest way to get rid of him for good.

Thirty years won't make a difference. Tell your buyer you'll sell.

The three little dots moved again but then disappeared. Showed again, but no words ever appeared.

Bang. Bang. Bang.

Stella knew that knock anywhere. Her father had obviously indulged before facing her. All these years, she'd thought she'd been the coward, but now she saw differently.

She rose and went to the door. "There's no reason for you to stay. There's no garage. It isn't yours."

"You can try to fight me, but I'll win in court." Her father's slurred words penetrated the metal door and years of distance between them.

"No need to fight. You can have the garage." She wouldn't

open the door, but she'd give him what he wanted and send him away.

"What?"

"It's yours."

He pounded on the door. "Then let me in."

"No need. You'll have to find a new location for the garage. This land is sold." She never thought she'd be so happy about letting this place go, but she knew her *abuelo* would approve to get her father out of her life.

Bang. Bang. Bang.

"What have you done, child? We could have sold the business and made some money. This isn't going to happen. I know it won't," he shouted through the door.

She held her palm to the cold metal between them, wishing their lives could've been different. That the man she knew as a young child would somehow conquer the man her father had become. It wouldn't happen, though. She held her cell phone close to her heart. If she had to call the sheriff, she would, but not unless there was no other way. He'd end up back in jail soon enough and out of her life.

"You think that boy of yours is so good? That you belong with him because he's rich and powerful? Well, news flash. Good. We'll have a constant source of income in our future."

Stella's breath caught somewhere between her lungs and her courage. No. She hadn't thought of that. He was right, though. If she stayed with Knox, her father would never leave them be.

"I hear you're restoring a 916 Porsche. Give that to me, and I'll be gone."

His words were like daggers piercing her resolve, but she cleared her throat and mustered the remnants of her courage. "No, you'll leave now."

"Fine, but I'll be back. You can't hide inside that place

forever. Besides, I have some friends who want to meet my beautiful daughter."

His words were like acid on her skin, eating away at her determination to forget that awful night. Her legs wobbled under her, so when she heard clomping down the old wooden steps, her legs collapsed and she slid to the floor, pulling her knees to her chest. She heaved and breathed through old night-mares and new ones forming. How did her father know about the 916? Had it been on the Internet? No, she'd looked through everything on the blog. It didn't matter. The truth of his words echoed through the empty garage. As long as she was with Knox, her father would never leave them alone. She shivered and shook as the room around her darkened, along with her newfound hope.

THIRTY

The man who didn't deserve to call himself a father backed away from the door at Knox's approach. "Can I help you with something, sir? If not, the sheriff can be here in minutes."

"No need. I'm done here for tonight." He stumbled and slid down the rocky parking lot.

"You need a lift? Out of town maybe?" Knox followed him, ready for a fight if need be. He trusted Stella to handle this, but when she didn't let her father in, Knox had assumed the sheriff was delayed. The woman was smart and capable, but everyone needed backup.

He spit when he shouted over his shoulder, "Be on your way, boy. This is my home."

Knox realized it was pointless to argue with a drunk, so he returned to his car and followed him to the stop sign at the edge of the town square, where he got into a vehicle with another man and they headed out of town.

Knox thought about returning to Stella, but then she'd think he didn't trust her to handle the situation, so he parked in the little space under the large oak trees at the edge of her parking lot, where he remained in the shadows for the rest of the night.

At the first sign of the orange light of the sun, he marched up to the garage door and knocked under the guise of visiting.

"Who's there?" her voice called through the door, as if she'd been sitting next to it all night. She sounded distant, tired. He didn't like feeling out of control and unable to make things better for her.

"It's Knox."

"I'm, ah...not decent at the moment. I wasn't expecting you so early."

He smiled at the thought. "No worries. I can wait."

"No. Don't," she snapped. "I mean, the sheriff is on his way here now, and this should all be over soon. You promised you wouldn't get involved."

"I'm not," he said, but the words were bitter. "Okay, I'll go, but I'll bring you some lunch in a couple of hours."

"No need. I'm meeting the girls for lunch. I'll catch up with you later."

Her words came fast and hard. Lies? No. Stella never lied. It was one of the things he loved about her. Her strength to always tell the truth, even if it hurt someone.

"Please, you have to go."

He didn't like the way her voice shook, but what could he do if she wouldn't let him inside. "Okay, I'm leaving, if you promise me one thing."

"What's that?"

He touched the door, willing her to open it and let him in. "If you need anything, you call or text me. I'm here for you if you want."

"You don't need to play hero."

He heard it. She was pushing him away and closing herself off to him. He couldn't let that happen. "I'm not. I'm your friend, and I care about you." He waited for a response, but when she didn't say anything, he knew his options were limited, so he returned to his car. There had to be something he could do. Ms. Horton would know, but she wasn't in town. He'd go hang out at the coffee shop and watch the road coming in and out of town. Perhaps he'd run into Stella when Mary-Beth went to meet her for lunch. He ached to see Stella. He needed to physically see that she was okay.

At Maple Grounds, he parked and went inside to find the sheriff at the register. Knox was thankful it wasn't crowded inside since it was early. "You headed to Stella's garage now?"

The sheriff raised an eyebrow at him. "Why would I be going there?"

Knox eyed him and then Mary-Beth. Was he keeping Stella's secret, or did he really not know? Knox backed away. "Sorry, my mistake. It's early and I need a cup of coffee."

Mary-Beth jumped into motion. "Coming right up."

When her back was turned, Knox snagged the sheriff's sleeve and pulled him away from the counter. The man looked down at his offending contact, but Knox ignored him. "It's okay. I know about Stella's father being in town and you going to hide and help her put him back in jail."

The sheriff pulled his sleeve free. "First of all, that sounds like entrapment. And second of all, I don't have a clue what you're talking about."

Knox eyed Mary-Beth, eyed the sheriff, eyed the door, but he didn't know what to do.

"You okay? I think all this work is getting to you. Maybe you need a break." The sheriff backed away from Knox as if *he* were the criminal.

Mary-Beth appeared at his side, holding a cup out to him. "What's wrong? You look like you've seen the legendary ghost of Sugar Maple pond."

"I don't know what to do," he mumbled. Perhaps Lori would know. No, she'd left town, too.

Mary-Beth adjusted her bracelets. "Tell me what's going on, and maybe I can help."

He thought about her words and the town, and that's when he realized Stella was strong and independent and he didn't want to change that about her, but this was harder than he'd thought it would be. He couldn't deny it any longer. He was a protector to his core, and he couldn't stand by while another woman was hurt on his watch. Friends... If Stella didn't want his help directly, he'd get the help of the town. "You don't have a lunch with Stella today, do you?"

"No." Mary-Beth tilted her head and her brow tightened.

"That's it. She can't do this on her own. Call the girls and get them here now, all except Stella."

"Why except Stella?" Mary-Beth asked.

The sheriff's radio crackled, and he took it outside before Knox could stop him.

"Please, I'll explain when the other girls are here." He felt like Mary-Beth had hooked him up with a caffeine IV and opened the drip wide.

"Actually, here comes Jackie now. I'll text Carissa and Felicia." Mary-Beth went to the back, so he turned his attention to Jackie.

"I need your help."

"I'm a popular woman today. Some stranger needed help this morning."

"Stranger? What did he want?" Knox wanted to run that man out of town, too. Maybe Stella was on to something and he really did need to play hero.

"He said he was a cousin of Stella's. Funny, I don't remember her having a cousin."

His muscles stiffened. That man wasn't her cousin. He knew it in his bones. "I need you to call a Fabulous Five Intervention."

Jackie narrowed her gaze. "What am I calling this intervention for?"

"To drive Stella's father out of town," he said but felt like he shouldn't have even shared that much. Stella's trust meant everything to him.

"He's in jail, last I heard. But if he wasn't, we wouldn't welcome him back to town. Not sure we need an entire town to help, though. We girls can handle it."

The front door opened, but he didn't take a breath to see who it was. "I know you don't like that I am in love with Stella, but you can't let your friend down because of that. She needs you."

"Love?" Jackie's chin rose and her shoulders went to attention.

He shook his head as if to clear it. "We can discuss my levels of feeling for her later. Right now, you need to go chase that man out of town. Get that sheriff back here and escort him out of here. Tar and southernize him if you have to."

"You believed that story?" Jackie laughed. "Tell me you won't do that to yourself to win Stella over. I don't think I could bear to see another man reduce himself to such tactics."

"You need to call the intervention now," he demanded.

"What's the intervention for?" Carissa approached with Drew and Felicia by her side.

Drew rushed to Knox. "What is it? I haven't seen you this riled since the war."

Knox's head spun, and he realized he was breathing fast and hard. "I need the girls club to get everyone to join forces to run Stella's father out of town. Come on, let's move."

"We can go to Stella's and tell him he isn't welcome here. What's the big deal?" Jackie demanded with a hint of irritation.

A car passed by outside. It was the car her father had taken out of town. There wasn't any more time. The sheriff wasn't at the garage. Knox wasn't there. No one was there to protect her.

"Her life is in danger."

They all looked at each other as if he'd gone mad.

"Don't you understand? It's her father. The man who went to jail."

"Yeah, for selling drugs and fraud. That doesn't mean he'd hurt Stella. He's still her father."

"He already did." Knox didn't have any more time to waste. He headed for the door, but Drew grabbed hold of him.

"How? Is he using again?" Mary-Beth asked from behind him.

"The man's an animal. Yes, I'm sure he's using." Knox didn't want to waste any more time arguing.

"If he's using, he won't hurt her." Mary-Beth's bracelets jingled at her approach. "He's only here to ask for money. We'll go by and check on Stella and cheer her up. No need to worry."

"Seriously, he's never hurt her before. We'd know." Jackie said with an air of irritation.

"He *is* a monster. He tried to sell her for drugs when she was a child!" He slammed his hand over his mouth, but it was too late. He'd betrayed Stella. He'd done the one thing he knew she'd never forgive him for: telling the world her darkest secret.

THIRTY-ONE

Stella shoved her last shirt into a bag, tied it, and dropped it next to the four boxes filled with her belongings. For now, she could stay at the inn with her earnings from the 916 Bradley had already paid. When Ms. Horton returned, Stella would request permission to keep the car and her tools in the old warehouse behind the recreation building. Once finished with the car, she'd receive the second half of the payment and she could figure out what was next.

One day at a time, one problem at a time like her *abuelo* would tell her. The car restoration episode for Knox would either have to be filmed elsewhere or be canceled, a realization that stabbed at her resolve, but he knew why she had to do this. Besides, she and Knox could never be together, not as long as her father was free.

Her body throbbed and protested every time she moved another box, not only from packing all night but at the realization she had to end things with Knox before they ever really began. How could her father always cost her so much? If only a few dollars would send him away for years instead of weeks, but he'd burn through everything the minute he found some drugs and women.

She wiped the sweat from her brow and abandoned the last of her packing to open a window. Daylight had come and with it a false sense of security. She'd spent all night mourning the loss of the garage and facing her fear of a man who no longer had power over her.

The boxes in the garage blocked the path to the door, so she stacked them near the Chevy and wheeled her tools near them. Once she finished packing, she'd call Felicia to borrow her truck and move her belongings to the county storage building for now. Hopefully Ms. Horton would understand her picking the lock—a skill she'd vowed at fifteen never to use again.

A car drove in, spitting rocks behind its tires and halting outside the door. She didn't even have to look to know her father had returned. It didn't matter. No more hiding.

She lifted the large garage door and stood on the threshold of her past and the obstacle to her future. "Hello, *Papa*."

The semisober, disheveled man who once bounced her on his knee stumbled around the car and faced her. He didn't look so frightening anymore. Not in daylight, and not with the years of abuse he'd done to himself.

Another man excited the vehicle, a young, handsome man with wide eyes who looked like he'd been dragged along instead of driven into this situation. Her father obviously had something on him to get him here. She pitied the man.

"I'm here to take my garage." He lifted his chin and marched up, halting a step from her, leaving little room to breathe.

Stella braced herself, shoulders back, despite still feeling like the little girl he'd dragged around like a puppet. "I'm assuming you were too drunk to remember our conversation last night."

He laughed and looked back at the stranger. "You hear that? Told you she was beautiful but not real bright." He stepped into her personal space. His stale beer and cigarette breath made her place her finger over her nose to keep from gagging.

"Why are you here? There's nothing for you. The garage is gone."

He laughed like a deranged clown. "You were paid a hunk of money for a car restoration. You want me gone, give me the money."

She felt like a thirteen-year-old girl: small, frightened...a child listening to authority despite the realization he was wrong. "No." Her voice sounded weak even to her, and based on the way his eyes softened, he'd found his opening.

The other man stayed in the periphery of her vision, and flashes of her being tugged into the barn that night, her father shouting *Look what I brought* echoed in her head. "You need to leave. Both of you."

"You think you're so special." He waved the other man closer, but the man didn't move. "This girl thinks Sugar Maple loves her. That she's better than her old man. Where are all your friends now?" He snorted. "Oh wait, that's right. One of your friends told us about the car, and another one told us about the show and what was going on in the town. So much for friendships."

"They wouldn't."

"They did." The man stepped forward, but when her father rounded on him and said, "Don't forget our deal," the man backed down.

She glanced at the door and regretted sending everyone away, but this was her battle and she'd finish it. "There is nothing for you here. You've got no ammo to use to get me to pay you anything."

The deep, guttural sound of his throat clearing, the noise he always made before he changed gears from reasonable to terrifying, echoed through the garage. He picked up a crowbar and swung it around like he was batting in the major leagues. "How well do you think the town will accept you when they find out you were trying to sell yourself for money?"

A fire erupted inside her. Years of anger and resentment raged. "I didn't. That was you!"

Her father swung the crowbar, landing a blow on the 916. A dent crushed into the front fender.

"Stop!"

"Then give me the money." He rested the crowbar on his shoulder.

The man with her father raced forward. "This isn't the way."

"Get out of my way." Her father's tone was dark and sinister. He had clearly hardened even more since she'd seen him last. She'd miscalculated his malice. The man hadn't improved but had deteriorated into a darker place.

The man didn't stop and blocked her father from the car. "No. I won't let you terrorize this woman."

"Then I'll just have to terrorize your mother instead."

The man lunged for her father.

Stella ran for her phone she'd left upstairs, but the sound of the crowbar hitting the man and the thump to the ground made her freeze a few steps from the stairs. She didn't want to, but she forced herself to look back and see the man on the ground holding his shoulder, moaning.

"No need to go run call your friends. They won't come. Besides, by the time they get here, I'll be gone." He didn't come after her, so she stayed at the bottom step.

She looked at the man and realized for the first time there was nothing left of the father she knew as a child. Despite what he'd tried to do to her, she'd still always held on to the hope the sober him would return. Now, she saw the truth. "You're a monster."

"A monster you made when you chased your mother away. Give me money. You owe me for sticking around."

Fury engulfed her reasoning, and she shot toward him. "I owe you nothing! Your cheating sent her away." She took in a stuttered breath, her eyes pricking with tears. "I never had parents. *Abuelo* and *abuela* were my only real family. You never loved me. All you both cared about was fame and fortune. When mom got out there she ditched you and you couldn't handle it so you turned to drinking and drugs. Apparently you weren't good enough either."

He raised the crowbar higher and stepped toward the stairs, but Stella didn't retreat. "Go ahead. I always knew you were a brute."

"Maybe I am." Instead of coming after her, he turned and went to the Chevy and raised the crowbar over his head. "Or maybe I'm just a disappointed father. This car was always more important than me. You and your grandfather lived for this thing instead of looking after me. If it weren't for you two, I wouldn't have been in jail for so long." He walked around the Chevy, studying it. "Give it to me to sell, or there won't be anything left of it for you to work on."

Knox walked in and halted a few steps inside. The expression on his face wasn't something she'd seen before. It was militaristic, combative, frightening. She wanted to throw her arms around him for coming to help but slap him for being there all at the same time. "Put down the crowbar now, or I'll forget I'm not supposed to be playing the hero."

THIRTY-TWO

A wildfire of rage consumed Knox at the sight of a man threatening Stella. It didn't matter that it was her father; the enemy needed to be dealt with.

"If it isn't white knight." Stella's father tossed down the crowbar. "I'm not doing anything illegal here. This is my car. Everything in this garage belongs to me." The way his gaze darted to Stella tossed gasoline on Knox's anger, catapulting him forward.

"But I was leaving." He didn't move his gaze from Stella. "For now."

"No, you won't be returning here ever again," Knox said firmly. "This is Stella's garage, and I'll make sure that you are never allowed back here."

"I won't be returning to the garage since apparently it's been sold. Of course, I demand any profits from the sale."

"Sold?" Knox captured the word, rolled it around in his head, but it didn't register. Stella would never sell her grandfather's garage.

Her father eyed him, then Stella, and then the door. "But I will visit my daughter on occasion. You can't stalk her all the time like you were last night in your car."

Stella moved into Knox's line of sight. "I told you to stay out of this."

He dared a glance at her, expecting to find anguish and fear, but it was more than that. The way she looked at him was distant. Her self-protected nature had returned, blocking him from any further emotional contact.

"Let me be clear." Knox ignored Stella's order to stay out of everything and marched over to face her father man-to-drunk. "You will never bother Stella again. You will no longer torture her or cause her pain. Not as long as I'm in her life."

"He's not in my life. Don't listen to him," Stella said, her words like napalm on his soul.

Knox thought he might double over in pain, but he knew he had to remain standing with no cracks showing in his façade to stand up to her father. He grappled for the rope of hope that she'd only said those words under some misguided attempt to protect him from her father. But if what she said was true, he still wanted to protect her. If he couldn't, her friends would.

Cars charged into the parking lot. The girls had done it. The entire town cavalry had arrived. If this didn't send the man running, nothing would. Jackie led the charge into the garage with the rest of the girls by her side. They rushed to Stella at the stairs and formed a human barrier.

"Mr. Frayser, Jackie said firmly, "you are no longer welcome in the town of Sugar Maple. We called the mayor, and she has spoken to the sheriff. You will be escorted out of town, and you will never return."

Stella blinked, mouth wide, scanning the crowd.

"You're all being manipulated by my daughter. You think she's so pure and innocent. She tried to sell herself when she was a kid, and I tried to protect her."

"No, you tried to sell her." Carissa spoke with more hatred

than Knox thought the girl was capable of possessing. "We know the truth, and your lies are not welcome here."

"How?" Stella asked in a small voice.

Knox knew this could destroy any chance they had to be together, but she needed to hear it from him. "I told them."

She gasped. "No."

"I told you. I'm the only one you can trust. That man only cares about himself." Her father marched toward the garage door. "I'll see you later, sweet girl."

Knox darted in front of him. "You're not going anywhere. The sheriff will be taking you into custody."

"For what?" He tossed the crowbar to the floor and held up his hands in an innocent shrug.

Knox went nose-to-nose with the man, ignoring his stench. "I'm sure you broke probation with your drinking. If not, I'll find another way to lock you up.'"

"I never touched my daughter," he snarled. "That's a line I wouldn't cross."

The man's deranged logic didn't compute, but it didn't matter.

The man on the floor managed to stand. "He smashed the 916 with a crowbar and assaulted me."

Stella's father lunged for him, but Knox grabbed his shoulders and wrapped him in a headlock. "Sheriff here yet?"

"I'm here." He came in, eyed the stranger across the room holding his shoulder, eyed the girls huddled on the stairs, and eyed Knox with the man Knox had in a headlock. "I'll take him to the station, and we can sort all this out there." He cuffed Stella's father and dragged him to the door.

"I'll be out in a day, and I'm sure your mother would love to see me," her father growled at the stranger.

Knox wanted to ask the man who he was and if he had anything to do with Stella's father being here, but instead he turned to face Stella, who was surrounded by her friends, who were holding her in a group hug.

"Stella." He crossed the room but stopped a few feet away. "I'm sorry. I didn't mean to hurt you."

"Get out. I trusted you." She slid between Felicia and Mary-Beth and looked down at him from the second step, her eyes wild, searching, angry, devastated. "But you betrayed me. You're a worse liar than my father."

Her words pierced his heart, his mind, his soul. The way she looked at him gave no room for doubt. They were over. She'd never get past the fact he'd broken her trust. And he didn't blame her. She lived, though. That's all that mattered. Even if they couldn't be together, he'd saved the girl in distress this time.

THIRTY-THREE

The girls settled in with pillows on Jackie's floor. Stella's stomach hadn't stopped swishing and whooshing since they'd discovered her secret. She felt dirty and nauseated and didn't want to be around anyone, but they insisted they had to stay together.

"Why didn't you tell us back then?" Carissa asked in her nonjudgmental way.

Stella squeezed the corner of the pillow and kept her eyes on the ground. "I don't know. Embarrassment? Shame? Even though nothing actually happened, I felt dirty, unwanted."

"What do you have to feel shameful about? It was your miserable excuse of a father who did that to you." Jackie surprised her with the support without even one snide remark. "Listen, I know we've had our differences, but I hope you know that I would've been by your side without question. We all would have."

Stella dared a peek at them all, and she didn't find the pitying looks she'd expected. "You guys know nothing actually happened. Ms. Horton rescued me. My father went to jail. I turned him over to the police and told them what happened, but thanks to Mr. Strickland having an investigator surrender evidence of fraud and dealing drugs, I never had to testify. I went to live with my grandparents and moved on with my life. It was as if it never happened, and that's what I wanted."

"We understand, but now it can be over because the secret is out and you can move on with your life, realizing no one judges you. That was fiction your father planted in your head at a young age." Felicia nudged closer but eyed the floor between them. "So why are you so angry at Knox?"

"I'm not." Stella toyed with the fringe on the edge of the pillow.

Mary-Beth moved up next to Felicia. "I don't understand. Then why did you say you were mad at him for telling us? You sent him away."

"We don't belong together. My life is not a good mix with his."

"You know your father manipulates. That's what he does. All addicts do that. I know. My mother went to treatment twice," Jackie said in a low, shameful tone.

They all stopped and looked at her.

"Oh, don't look so surprised. You were there at the Christmas party at school in tenth grade when she fell down drunk and knocked over the nativity scene."

"You said she tripped. You ushered her out so quickly, stating she was hurt, that we didn't know." Carissa reached out across the circle to Jackie, despite their rift that had closed but not mended completely over the last few months.

Jackie took Carissa's hand, squeezed it, and then retreated. It was progress. Maybe Jackie wasn't a fashionista robot after all.

She shifted her pillow under her chest but then redirected attention back to Stella. "Anyway... You obviously fell for Knox. You shouldn't walk away so easily. I hate to admit it, but that man tamed you, something I failed at years ago."

"You're right. And he deserves better than what I can give him," Stella whispered.

Everyone started talking, saying she was wrong, until Jackie bolted upright. "Oh no, you don't."

Stella looked up at her. "Don't what?"

"You're pushing Knox away out of some false sense that you're protecting him. What did your father threaten? Have you learned nothing from all this? Your father has no power over you any longer. We won't let him. *Knox* won't let him."

Stella shrugged. "He's better off without me. You know my father is never going to rest until he gets what he wants, which is fame. He'll take to any media he can to play the father of the woman who snagged Knox Brevard and then twist it for any sick purpose he can for money."

Felicia toyed with the end of Stella's hair, as if fixing a wayward curl. "You know, the man Declan—the one with your father—told me your dad has been obsessed with you and your success since he first heard about you being on the Knox Brevard show. He says he's willing to testify to put him in jail, which means he won't be able to bother you and Knox anymore."

"Why are you talking to a convict?" Jackie snipped at Felicia.

"He's not a convict. The man was only trying to get her father away from his mother. He'd been terrorizing her. Declan thought they were done with him when he went to prison, but then he returned. He's a good person, only trying to protect his family."

"Oh, no. Felicia picked up another stray," Jackie quipped.

Felicia waved her away and smashed the pillow under her to sit up higher, speaking directly to Stella. "He told me that you should go face your father and tell him you won't let him manipulate you anymore. At least speak to him before you abandon Knox."

Stella wiggled down and flipped over, pulling the blanket to her chin. "I'll sleep on it."

Jackie dimmed the lights. "We all know that means that Stella is done talking, so let's get some beauty rest. You all need it."

"Good night," Felicia said, followed by the rest. It sounded like a rerun of *The Waltons*, Sugar Maple style.

They all settled into sleep quickly, except Stella. She stared at the ceiling for hours, contemplating facing her father. She knew she needed to, if for no other reason than she'd be able to sleep again, knowing he was behind bars. She slipped out before any of the girls woke up and insisted on going with her. They meant well and she loved them for it, but she didn't want the company. Despite being upset with Knox, she missed him already. A part of her wanted to do the show with him. Her life felt full of possibilities when he was around, but if she truly cared about him, how could she expose him to her complicated life? If he was anything like her parents, he'd eventually leave for fame anyway.

She walked through town and out the other side, enjoying the spring air. The sheriff's car parked in front of the station indicated she'd be able to get in this early. Good thing the sheriff's office and jail were small-town size so there wasn't a lot of red tape to deal with to visit someone.

Inside, she found the sheriff hunched over the front desk. "Good morning. How are you doing today, Stella?"

"I'm okay. My father still here?" she asked, as if discussing the spring heat wave expected this week.

"Yep. You want to see him? He's sobered up and quieter than when I put him in the cell. I'd feel sorry for him if it wasn't for how he treated you."

"He has that effect on people." She recalled how many times she'd given him her money from doing odd jobs around town and babysitting because they needed food or he needed a drink.

Her chest tightened at the sight of the door. The sound of the metal slamming shut behind her made her jump. The odor of cleaning chemicals with an undertone of sweat and bodily fluids did nothing to calm her stomach. She hadn't been in a jail since that night so many years ago. A child with a blanket wrapped around her, shivering in the corner. That was the night she decided to be brave and strong and never need to be taken care of again.

"Hey, you've got a visitor," the sheriff called through the cell ahead.

Stella took in a sharp breath, pushed back her shoulders, and marched to the bars. "Tell me the truth. Why did you come? How did you get out of jail?"

He sat up on his hip, rubbing his head and groaning. "I didn't mean to cause you any pain, sweet girl."

"Don't call me that."

He looked through his long gray bangs at her and then flipped the hair onto his head. "I came to be with you. I'll do better. I'll go back to NA, and we can work in the garage together. You know your grandfather taught me a lot about cars."

"I told you the garage isn't mine anymore. The land sold. I'm moving out and moving on with my life."

"You mean with that man that will only stick around long enough to poison you against me and use you for his show and then leave?"

"That's you, not Knox." Did she believe her own words? Knox hadn't run off when things got tough. He'd stayed and protected her, despite her sending him away. "You haven't changed a bit. You're still blaming everyone else. You'll never take responsibility for your actions." Stella backed away. "I don't know why I came."

"Because you're my daughter." He shot up with a wobble. "You can't trust anyone but me. I always told you only to trust family."

"You didn't have to choose to do drugs and terrorize me again. Yes, you're family. The father I once knew. But the one who taught me to throw a baseball, slug a boy, and sat up all night with me when I had the chicken pox doesn't exist anymore. He died when I was a child, and it's time for me to finally let him go."

"What are you going to do? Run to the man who will never choose you over his show?" Her father spit his words through the bars.

"No. I'll take care of myself. I don't need anyone to take care of me. You taught me that."

"I know, sweet girl. You're so strong that you could help me get clean. Post bail and take me to a meeting." He grasped the bars and pushed his head as far as it could go through them.

"You're the only one who can get you clean." A shooting star of realization crossed her mind. The man on the other side of the bars was responsible for his own actions, and he chose time and time again to abandon Stella, but Knox, the man who'd brought the entire town to her aide, had stayed by her side, despite the possibility of bad press.

"You'll be back when that guy leaves. He's a loser like them all."

"No. He's a hero. *My* hero."

THIRTY-FOUR

"Go talk to her." Lori tossed her bag onto the coffee table in the inn's parlor and plopped down at Knox's side.

He rubbed his chest, trying to free it of the ache that hadn't let go since Stella had walked out of his life. "No. I won't put her through any more. I told the town her secret. How could she ever forgive me? *I* wouldn't forgive me."

Lori patted his knee. "Yes, you would, because you like her. You like her a ton. I think you're falling in love with her."

"Maybe I am. Because there was a time I'd fight for what I wanted. Now, I care more about what's right for her. And I'm not it." He pushed up from the sofa and headed out the front door. "I hate to tell you, but you're going to have some damage control to handle. Drew only has a week left working with us, and then we're on our own." He paused at the door, the realization that his decision to walk away from the streaming deal hadn't only impacted himself, but also Lori. "I'm sorry that I passed on the streaming deal. I should've consulted with you prior to telling Bradley no."

"It was the right thing to do, especially since you didn't

make that decision for selfish reasons. I know you did it for Stella."

"After what happened with the 916, Bradley wasn't so interested in working with either of us anyway. From what I've heard Stella has been working day and night on his car to fix it." He shut the door before Lori could provide any more unsolicited advice.

The town had resumed their normal activities, but instead of feeling like an outsider walking down the street, he felt like a Sugar Maplean. He knew names and faces, and everyone waved at him. He liked it. Too bad he couldn't stay.

"Hey, Knox. You gonna meet for poker tonight at the rec center?" Martin, the town grocer, asked.

A day ago, Knox would've welcomed the opportunity to fit into the community more, but not now. "I'd love to, but I have to work."

Davey shuffled up the sidewalk. "All work and no play makes Knox a duller boy than he already is." He patted Knox on the back. "Let me buy you a cup of coffee."

Since when did Davey buy anything for anyone? "Ah, sure."

Knox didn't know how to turn the man down. It was such an honor to be invited to sit with him by the town elder who hated all outsiders. "Thanks."

Knox jogged ahead and opened the door to Maple Grounds, but Davey shuffled past.

"Um, I thought we were getting coffee."

"We are, but not here. What, you think I'm old and can't remember where the coffee is? Come with me."

The owner of the general store ran up the hill ahead of them. Who knew the man could even run, considering he usually walked with a limp and grimace... The woman who drove the school bus ducked behind a tree and then shot across the road.

"What's going on? Why are we headed up the road toward Stella's garage?"

"Told ya, we're going for coffee. Don't you listen? Turn on your hearing aid."

At the edge of the side road, Jake came out side on the front porch and waved. It was progress. From what he'd overheard in town, Jake had been seen sitting in his garden twice. Hopefully, he could get Jake to meet him for coffee before he had to leave Sugar Maple.

Knox was worried Davey wouldn't make it up the hill. To Knox's surprise, despite the man walking at the speed of a turtle, he didn't stumble once. "I don't think I'm welcome at the garage."

"Why? You paid of the garage rent up-to-date and then some so Stella could stay," Davey announced.

"Wait, what? How'd you find that out?" Knox scanned the area, waiting for Stella to throw something at him. "You can't tell Stella."

They reached the gravel drive, and Davey stopped. "That's not a good way to start a life with one of my girls. She's special and you don't deserve her, but get your butt in there before I have to knock some sense into you." Davy pushed up his sleeves and held lifted his fists.

Knox stifled a laugh and noticed the commotion inside the garage. Curiosity tugged him across the lot and inside, where he found Drew, Carissa, and most of the town. "What's going on here?"

Stella stepped out in her white, hip-hugging dress. A knot formed in his throat at the sight of the most beautiful person he'd ever seen. The thought he could never feel her touch, or taste her lips again seared his heart with more pain than a bullet to his chest.

The crowd silenced and didn't move. She took a deep breath

and approached him with wide eyes and stiff posture. "I realize that I'm a private person and I don't like people knowing anything about me, but I don't mind them knowing about you."

Knox scanned the room and spotted a smiling Ms. Horton and Mr. Strickland, Felicia standing next to the man who'd been hit in the shoulder with the crowbar, and so many others. "I don't understand."

She crossed the room and took both of his hands sending a zap of pleasure through his body. "I'm glad you told my friends the truth about my past."

His breath caught. "I thought you hated me..." Knox searched her face for the answer.

"I don't. I thought I was pushing you away to protect you from my father."

He puffed out his chest. "I'm not scared of him."

"I know that. I also know that wasn't the only reason. I'm afraid that even though I didn't believe it deep inside, I did push you away because I was scared that you'd care more about fame than about me. It wasn't fair to you, and I'm sorry. I don't expect you to accept my apology, but I wanted the world to know that you aren't a stranger from out of town meant to hurt me and destroy all the sweetness of Sugar Maple but that you're a hero. One who should be welcomed anytime." Stella squeezed his hands tight and took in another long breath. "I realize I've messed up. I know you didn't mean to tell anyone my secret, but I'm glad you did. The pressure of keeping that all these years is finally gone. I feel happy and hopeful, and that's because of you. You chose me over your show when you called the town together to save me. I mean, that could've been front page news tomorrow." Her voice cracked.

His heart beat like a timpani drum at a carnival. Could she have really forgiven him? Did she still care for him? "You mean more to me than any show."

"If you want to tell the world about us, we have a set ready to go. We'll do another special message to your fans, and I'll help you with whatever show you want to run. Please, just tell me that you forgive me or tell me what I can do to make this right."

"Nothing," he blurted, looking into her eyes and seeing the strong, beautiful, caring, and compassionate woman like he'd never seen her before. "Because there's nothing to forgive."

He couldn't hold himself back any longer, so he wrapped his arms around her and pulled her tight, kissing her with all the love he could pour into her. A kiss to seal them together. A kiss to tell her how much he cared.

Her body melted into his, as if she fully opened her heart to him, and lowered her wall of fear. He relished the moment. A real moment of true connection with a woman who turned him around, challenged him every moment they were together, and had awoken a part of him he thought had died years ago.

The townspeople of Sugar Maple hooted and hollered their approval. He felt adored. Not from the cheers of a crowd in the superficial way of stardom, but in a real, warmth in your bones kind of way. Because Stella didn't make him feel lost and alone, but for the first time in many years, he felt alive. Alive and loved.

The End

If you would like to continue your journey through Sugar Maple, please click here.

ABOUT THE AUTHOR

Ciara Knight is a USA TODAY Bestselling Author, who writes clean and wholesome romance novels set in either modern day small towns or wild historic old west. Born with a huge imagination that usually got her into trouble, Ciara is happy she's found a way to use her powers for good. She loves spending time with her characters and hopes you do, too.

ALSO BY CIARA KNIGHT

For a complete list of my books, please visit my website at www.
ciaraknight.com. A great way to keep up to date on all releases, sales
and prizes subscribe to my Newsletter. I'm extremely sociable, so feel
free to chat with me on Facebook, Twitter, or Goodreads.

For your convenience please see my complete title list below, in
reading order:

CONTEMPORARY ROMANCE

Winter in Sweetwater County

Spring in Sweetwater County

Summer in Sweetwater County

Fall in Sweetwater County

Christmas in Sweetwater County

Valentines in Sweet-water County

Fourth of July in Sweetwater County

Thanksgiving in Sweetwater County

Grace in Sweetwater County

Faith in Sweetwater County

Love in Sweetwater County

Sugar Maple Series

If You Love Me

If You Adore Me

If You Cherish Me

If You Hold Me

If You Kiss Me

Riverbend

In All My Wishes

In All My Years

In All My Dreams

In All My Life

A Christmas Spark

A Miracle Mountain Christmas

HISTORICAL WESTERNS:

McKinnie Mail Order Brides Series

Love on the Prairie

(USA Today Bestselling Novel)

Love in the Rockies

Love on the Plains

Love on the Ranch

His Holiday Promise

(A Love on the Ranch Novella)

Love on the Sound

Love on the Border

Love at the Coast

A Prospectors Novel

Fools Rush

Bride of America

Adelaide: Bride of Maryland

YOUNG ADULT:

Battle for Souls Series

Rise From Darkness

Fall From Grace

Ascension of Evil

The Neumarian Chronicles

Weighted

Escapement

Pendulum

Balance

Made in the USA
Las Vegas, NV
30 August 2022